Curvy, Curvy, Curvy, Dr Belle. MD

The Plus Size Women Books

Cherry Hargrove, Author

Chapters

PREFACE

Some stories begin with certainty.
This one begins with breath.

In this series of 1890 women plus size doctors, Dr. Belle is the story of a woman who survives before she is celebrated, who serves before she is believed, and who learns that obedience often looks nothing like approval. It is a frontier story, but not one defined by land alone. It is about bodies that carry memory, faith that grows in quiet places, and healing that moves through hands long before it is understood.

Belle does not arrive in the West as a conqueror or a heroine. She arrives bruised, displaced, misunderstood, and still breathing. What follows is not a straight path upward, but a winding road through wilderness, compassion, rejection, obedience, and purpose. The people she encounters are often the ones history overlooks or misunderstands, yet they become her teachers as much as her patients.

This book is not about perfection. It is about calling that persists when reputation fails. It is about faith that moves when comfort disappears. It is about the God who works not only through institutions and approval, but through kitchens, camps, wagons, fields, and women who refuse to disappear.

If you have ever felt delayed rather than defeated, unseen rather than unworthy, or uncertain yet still obedient, this story is for you. May it remind you that survival is not shameful, obedience is rarely tidy, and being "still breathing" is sometimes the holiest place to begin.

What you will read here in this book is called *"grace"*.

CHAPTER ONE

Still Breathing

She had been curvy since childhood—not the awkward kind, not the apologetic sort, but the kind that filled a doorway with warmth before she ever spoke. Golden hair that refused to lie flat spilled down her back in soft rebellion, and her laughter—oh, her laughter—came out of her like a hymn she never meant to sing but could never quite keep inside.

On the dairy farm where she was raised, no one ever told her to shrink.

The cows did not care.
The horses did not notice.
The chickens scattered regardless of her shape.

Her father used to say the land made room for everything God intended to thrive, and her mother would smile and add that the same must be true of people. She grew into her body among wide skies and open fields, milk pails clanging in rhythm with her steps, laughter ringing against the barn walls while dawn still clung to the grass.

She learned early how to tend a creature that could not speak for itself. A limping mare taught her patience. A feverish calf taught her care. A stubborn rooster taught her when to stand her ground. By twelve, she knew how to soothe a frightened animal, how to clean a wound, how to mix a poultice that actually worked. By fourteen, neighbors quietly brought her their sick livestock when the men's remedies failed.

She never thought of it as a calling. It was simply what needed doing.

Henry College came later—almost unbelievably later—an opportunity that felt like a door no farm girl was meant to open. But she did. She studied medicine not with bitterness, but with joy. Anatomy fascinated her. Physiology made sense. Healing, when taught properly, felt like learning the language God had already written into the body.

She was curvy there, too.

Curvy in lecture halls.
Curvy walking between classes.
Curvy while outperforming men who underestimated her.

Her humor carried her through the whispers. Her confidence unsettled professors who weren't sure what to do with a woman who laughed easily and learned quickly. She earned her medical license honestly, deliberately, brilliantly. And because she loved nourishment as much as healing, she pursued culinary training alongside it—learning not just how to cook, but how to feed with intention, how food could restore a weakened body as much as any tonic.

She left Henry with certificates that proved her competence—but no guarantee of welcome.

The railroad promised freedom. It promised towns desperate for doctors, places where no one would care what her body looked like if she saved their children or their livestock.

CHAPTER TWO

Belle of the Barn

Annabelle Foster had been born laughing.

At least that's what her father always said.

"She came out smiling like she'd heard a joke before the rest of us," he liked to tell the neighbors, wiping his hands on his overalls. "Curviest little bundle I ever saw. Lord help the chairs she'll sit on when she's grown."

"Henry," her mother would scold, though her eyes always shone, "you leave that girl alone. The Lord doesn't make mistakes, and He certainly didn't start with your daughter."

From the time she could toddle through the barn, Belle filled the dairy farm with motion—soft blonde hair bouncing, skirts swishing, laughter chasing the chickens into indignant retreat.

One hot afternoon when she was about eight, she marched into the kitchen, hands on her little hips, cheeks pink from pumping water.

"Mama," she announced, "the cows like me better than they like Papa."

Her mother, Clara, turned from the stove, where a pot of stew was bubbling. "Do they now, Miss Annabelle?"

"Yes ma'am. When Papa comes with the milk pail they stare at him like he owes them money. When I come, they flick their ears and line up proper. I think the Lord gave me a special gift with cows."

Her father leaned in through the open back door just in time to hear. "More like you bribe 'em with your talking. You chatter 'til they're too confused not to cooperate."

Belle lifted her chin. "The Bible says a gentle tongue can break a bone, Papa. Maybe my gentle tongue just—just softens udders."

Her mother choked on a laugh and had to turn back to the stew, shaking her head. "Don't you dare say that again in front of Pastor Whitcomb."

"Yes ma'am," Belle said, but the sparkle in her eyes said she absolutely would.

Growing Up Curvy

By twelve, Belle had hips, curves, and opinions. The opinions concerned her mother more than the rest.

One Sunday as they walked back from church, Belle caught snippets of ladies whispering on the road behind them.

"Pretty face… shame about the size…"
"Gets it from Henry's side, surely, Clara keeps a clean kitchen…"

Belle's shoulders dipped. Her mother heard it too. She slowed her steps and slipped an arm around Belle's waist.

"Look at me, Annabelle."

Belle glanced up.

"Is the Lord displeased with those cows because they're well-fed?"

"No, ma'am."

"Does He scold the wheat for growing thick and tall instead of skinny and sick?"

"No."

"Then why would He be displeased that He made you strong instead of fragile?"

Belle blinked fast. "I just… I wish I didn't take up so much of the pew."

Henry cleared his throat ahead of them. "Well I wish I didn't take up so much of my britches, but here we all are." He turned around and walked backward for a few steps, grinning at her. "You listen to your mama, girl. The Lord doesn't carve twigs when He's building oaks."

Belle laughed in spite of herself. "Papa, I can't be an oak. Oaks got bark."

"You already got bark," he said. "I've heard you when that rooster won't mind you."

Her mother swatted him with her Bible. "Henry Foster!"

He dodged and winked at Belle. "Anyway, if folks are busy watching how big you are, they won't notice how big your mind is 'til it's too late. Then you'll out-think 'em and take their money—politely."

"Papa!" Belle giggled.

Clara squeezed her. "You be kind, Annabelle. But don't you ever apologize for existing. You understand?"

"Yes ma'am," Belle said softly. "I'll try."

"Don't just try," her father said. "Live."

9

The Essay

When the Henry College essay contest was announced in the county paper, Belle read it three times at the breakfast table.

"'An essay of no more than one thousand words describing how higher education can serve rural communities,'" she read aloud. "Mama, do you suppose they mean our kind of rural, or the fancy kind where they have sidewalks?"

Clara wiped her hands on her apron. "Words are words, baby. Rural is rural. You thinking of entering?"

"For a scholarship?" Henry asked, lowering his coffee cup. "That's all the way up in Ohio. They won't take cows as tuition."

Belle folded the paper carefully. "It says women can study there… and colored students… and people who aren't rich." Her heart thumped. "Maybe they'd take a curvy farm girl who knows how to keep a calf alive."

Her father studied her face. "You really want to go?"

Belle nodded. "I want to learn how the body works so I can fix it proper. I'm tired of guessing at poultices and praying I don't make someone worse."

"Prayer's not guessing," Clara said gently, "but I know what you mean."

Henry sighed, long and slow. "Write your essay then."

Belle blinked. "Just like that?"

"Just like that," he said. "If the Lord opens a door, we don't argue over the hinges. We walk through."

That night, by lamplight, Belle wrote until her hand cramped. She wrote about the old farmer whose infected cut almost cost him his arm, and the baby calf she'd saved when the vet declared it hopeless, and the neighbor woman who died in childbirth because there was no doctor near who respected women's bodies.

She wrote about how knowledge could turn panic into practice, fear into treatment, ignorance into mercy.

Her mother found her at the table near midnight.

"You still at it, baby?"

"Just finishing." Belle sanded the ink and smiled. "If they don't like this, then they don't deserve my curves at their school."

"I don't think you're supposed to threaten the judges," Clara said, but she kissed her daughter's hair anyway.

Weeks later, the letter came.

Belle opened it on the front steps with trembling fingers. Her parents hovered, pretending not to hover.

"'Dear Miss Annabelle Foster,'" she read aloud. "'We are pleased to inform you that your essay has been awarded first place in the rural scholarship competition…'"

She broke off, shrieking, and the rest of the words scattered as she flung herself at her parents.

"I told you," Henry said, his voice suspiciously thick. "Henry doesn't know what's about to hit it."

Henry

The first thing Belle noticed about Henry College was how many people there were. People with books, people with ideas, people with opinions they said out loud as if no one would punish them for it.

The second thing she noticed was how narrow most of the benches were.

"I swear," she whispered to her new roommate on the first day, "these seats were built by dried-up men who only ever sat with dictionaries."

Her roommate, Ruth, snorted into her handkerchief. "If you keep talking like that, you'll be sent home."

"They'll have to find a seat big enough to launch me first," Belle said.

Ruth, a serious-looking girl from Cleveland with dark braids and round glasses, warmed quickly to Belle's humor. They shared a room in a drafty dormitory with two other young women—Naomi, a poised Black student from Cincinnati studying literature, and Mei, a quiet, sharp-eyed woman from California who was determined to become a teacher.

On their first night, Belle flopped onto her bed with a melodramatic sigh.

"Well, ladies, we are officially women of learning. How does everyone feel?"

"Terrified," Ruth said.

"Underestimated," Naomi added. "Which is my favorite starting position."

Mei looked thoughtful. "I feel… responsible," she said slowly. "If they are foolish enough to admit us, we must be wise enough to use it."

Belle grinned. "I feel hungry. But I suppose we can be responsible while I eat."

Professors and Opinions

Medical lectures were dense, long, and filled with men who had never milked a cow in their lives.

One afternoon, Professor Bartlett, a tall, stiff man with a moustache like a broom, tapped a diagram of the human heart with his cane.

"The female heart," he declared, "being more delicate, is particularly susceptible to hysteria and emotional excess. Women, therefore, must avoid strain, intellectual exertion, and—"

He faltered. Belle had snorted out loud.

"Miss Foster?" he said sharply. "You find something amusing?"

"Yes, sir," Belle said, cheeks pink but eyes bright. "I was just thinking if women's hearts were that delicate, we'd all be dead by twenty. My mama's heart has survived childbirth, drought, and my father's fiddle playing. If that isn't proof of structural integrity, I don't know what is."

Snickers rippled across the room. Naomi covered her mouth. Ruth stared at the ceiling. Mei's eyes sparkled.

Professor Bartlett stiffened. "We will refrain from anecdotes and focus on science."

"Yes, sir," Belle said, but she caught Naomi's eye and stage-whispered, "I thought I was focusing on science. That's field research where I come from."

Later, outside, Naomi looped her arm through Belle's.

"You are going to get us all expelled," she said, laughing.

"Not until I pass anatomy," Belle said. "Then they can't un-teach me what I know."

Culinary Side Quest

Belle's interest in food turned from necessity to art after she wandered into the domestic science kitchen by accident one rainy afternoon.

The instructor, Mrs. Haversham, eyed her skeptically. "This is an advanced class, dear. Are you sure you're in the right place?"

"Probably not," Belle said cheerfully, "but I saw bread and followed it. I'm studying medicine, but if I'm going to be fixing people, I'd like to know how not to poison them at dinner."

Mrs. Haversham snorted in spite of herself. "Can you cook anything?"

"I can make a stew that'll make a man apologize without knowing why," Belle said.

"Aprons are on the hooks," the woman said. "Don't get flour on the ceiling."

Belle learned quickly that there was chemistry in the kitchen, too—ratios and reactions, heat and time working together. She loved it. Loved the way a handful of ingredients could become comfort. Loved the way food thawed suspicion and softened scowls.

She started feeding her roommates.

"I swear your biscuits could end wars," Ruth said one evening, crumbs on her chin.

"My biscuits could at least stall hostilities until dessert," Naomi added.

"Food is proof that God likes us and wants us to stop arguing," Belle said, passing the butter.

The Job Announcement

It was Naomi who smoothed the notice flat on the library table one crisp spring afternoon.

"Look at this," she said. "A town out west. Cedar Ridge. Territory, not state yet. They're looking for a physician. They say they'll 'consider' a woman if she comes with references."

Belle looked up from her notes. "A woman doctor? Out west?" Her heart thumped.

Ruth peered over Naomi's shoulder. "Says here: 'Frontier community in need of medical practitioner. Lodging and modest salary provided. Must be willing to treat both townspeople and travelers.'"

Mei pointed to the bottom. "And there— 'persons of strong moral character preferred.'" She smiled faintly. "That's you, Belle. Strong moral character and stronger coffee."

Belle read the notice twice, three times. Buildings flickered in her imagination—rough boardwalks, dusty streets, horses tied to hitching posts. A place that needed her, really needed her, not just as a curiosity but as a lifeline.

"I could go," she whispered.

"You should go," Naomi said. "They'll probably try to pay you in chickens, but you should go."

Ruth chewed her lip. "It's dangerous, Belle."

"So is staying where no one expects anything of me but jokes and biscuits," Belle said. "Out there, they might not care what size I am as long as their fever breaks."

Naomi squeezed her hand. "Write to them. Send Professor Bartlett's grudging recommendation. He'll never admit you're smarter than he is, but he'll vouch that you passed his course."

"And Mrs. Haversham's letter," Mei added. "If they don't value your food, they don't deserve your medicine."

Belle laughed. "Imagine their faces when they realize their doctor can also bake."

"Frontier revival," Naomi said. "Souls healed by sermons, bodies healed by medicine, tempers healed by pie."

"Now that," Belle said, "sounds like a practice I'd like to run."

Saying Yes

Within weeks, invitations turned into a formal offer. Cedar Ridge wanted her.

"We have no doctor currently in residence," the town's letter read. "We are prepared to offer lodging above the general store, a fair salary, and… the gratitude of our people."

During her brief vacation back home, Her father read it aloud at the kitchen table, his voice slow and careful.

"Well," he said at last, "sounds like they're serious."

Her mother folded her hands tightly. "It's so far," she murmured. "And the West is… wild."

Belle reached for her mother's fingers. "Mama, the Lord's already out there. I won't be the first person to trust Him past the county line."

Henry cleared his throat. "You sure you're ready for this, Belle? There's no shame in saying 'not yet.'"

She looked between them—not as a girl begging permission but as a woman weighing calling.

"I've been reading about the towns out there," she said. "They've got accidents and births and fevers just like we do—only fewer people trained to help. If I stay here, I'll always wonder whose life I could have saved if I'd gone."

Clara's eyes shone. "You always were the child who tried to fix every broke wing on this farm."

Belle smiled. "Maybe it's time I tried fixing some farther out."

Henry leaned back with a sigh that seemed to come from his boots. "Then we'd best start packing," he said. "Can't let the West think we raised you without a decent coat."

Goodbye at the Station

The morning she left, the sky was the pale pink of a shy promise. The small station swarmed with people—some traveling, some just watching the train as if it were a visiting relative.

Belle stood with her valise in one hand and her medical bag in the other, hat pinned firmly over her blonde curls. Her curves made the traveling suit a little snug, but she refused to be ashamed of taking up space on the platform.

Henry fussed with the buttons on her coat. "Don't let strangers carry your bag unless they look too weak to steal it," he said.

"Yes, Papa."

"Don't skip meals. You get mean when you're hungry."

"Papa."

"And if some fellow out there thinks he can tell you what you can't do, you tell him you passed anatomy and can locate his foolishness on a chart."

Belle laughed. "Yes, Papa."

Clara's hands trembled as she adjusted Belle's collar. "You write as soon as you get there," she said. "And before. And after. And in between."

"I will, Mama." Belle swallowed. "You sure you're all right with this?"

"No," Clara said honestly. "But I love the Lord, and I love you, and sometimes those two loves mean letting go sooner than I'd like." She cupped Belle's face. "Just promise me one thing."

"What's that?"

"Promise me you'll pray when you're scared, not just when you're brave."

Belle's throat tightened. "Yes, ma'am. I promise."

The whistle blew, high and urgent.

Henry pulled Belle into a fierce hug, smelling of hay and pipe smoke and home. "You go make us proud, Annabelle Foster," he whispered. "And remember—no matter how far you go, you're never out of God's reach."

She hugged them both once more, heart aching and swelling all at once, then turned toward the train.

"Lord," she whispered under her breath as she climbed the steps, "I have no idea what I'm doing. But You do. So… please walk ahead of me, behind me, and on both sides, and if I wander, nudge me before I get stupid. In Jesus' name, amen."

She stepped into the car.

On the Railroad

The westbound coach was crowded and lively, full of people who looked as though they had packed their last chance along with their baggage. Belle wrestled her valise into the overhead rack with less grace than she would have liked.

"Need a hand, miss?" a lanky young man asked, half rising from his seat.

"I need a taller shelf," she puffed, finally shoving the bag into place. "But I'll accept your compliment to my independence."

He blinked, then laughed. "Name's Tom Jenkins. Heading to Kansas to be a telegraph operator."

"Annabelle Foster," she said. "Heading to somewhere past Kansas to be a doctor."

His eyebrows shot up. "A doctor? You?"

"Why not me?" she said lightly. "I'm big enough to block the Grim Reaper in a doorway."

The older woman across the aisle chuckled. "Well, we'll be safe then, won't we?" she said. "I'm Mrs. Gray, going to live with my daughter in Missouri. She just had a baby and her husband's about as useful as a fence made of string."

Belle grinned. "Then the Lord has orchestrated this nicely. I catch babies and criticize useless men as part of my training."

Mrs. Gray's eyes crinkled. "You a praying woman, Miss Foster?"

"Try to be," Belle said. "Some days it's more like complaining politely to the Almighty, but He hasn't struck me down yet."

Tom chuckled. "You always talk like this?"

"Only when I'm awake," Belle said.

The train lurched forward. The station slid away—her parents, her town, the life she'd known shrinking into a blur.

Belle sat back, heart thudding. For a moment, fear tried to crawl up her spine and settle in her chest.

She bowed her head.

"Lord," she prayed silently, "thank You for this ridiculous train, for the man who invented it, and for whoever decided to let women ride it without supervision. Please take care of Mama and Papa. Keep this train on the tracks and my nerves anchored to You. And if You could put me near people who don't snore like dying hogs, I would count it as special favor. Amen."

She opened her eyes to find Mrs. Gray watching her kindly.

"You just have a word with the Lord there, dear?" the older woman asked.

"Yes, ma'am."

"Good. We're going to need it. Men and machines, you know." She nodded toward Tom. "No offense."

"None taken," he said. "I don't trust either."

As the hours passed, Belle traded stories with her fellow passengers. She described milking cows in winter and how a frozen tail in the face could make a theologian out of anyone. Mrs. Gray told tales of her daughter's courtship, complete with the time the poor fellow had fainted during a proposal thanks to a tight collar.

Tom confessed he was more comfortable with wires than people. "Telegraphs don't talk back," he said.

"Neither do cows," Belle replied, "but I've seen them judge."

Laughter traveled the length of the car more than once. When a toddler began to cry, Belle entertained him by making faces and pretending her hat could talk. When a nervous young woman fretted aloud about leaving home, Belle squeezed her hand.

"Jesus left home too," she said. "He understands. And He didn't even have a return ticket."

Night fell, and the lamps lit the car in a warm, flickering glow. The train rattled on, steady and relentless.

Belle rested her head against the window, watching darkness swallow the fields.

"Lord," she murmured, so quietly no one could hear, "if I've misheard You… if I'm charging in the wrong direction… please make it clear before I ruin anything important. But if this is where You want me, then I'm trusting You to meet me at the other end of these tracks."

Her reflection in the glass looked back at her: curvy, blonde, tired, hopeful.

"Still breathing," she whispered to herself. "Still Yours."

Outside, the vast unknown stretched ahead—wild, untamed, waiting.

She smiled.

Whatever came next, she wasn't facing it alone.

CHAPTER THREE

The Eye of the Storm

Annabelle Foster had counted the days carefully.

Seven more days of travel, that was what the schedule had promised. Seven days of rattling tracks, shared stories, cramped seats, and lukewarm coffee from tin pots at waystations. Seven days between everything she had ever known and everything she had not yet seen.

The train had been her moving world—cars clanking together like an argument that never quite resolved, passengers coming and going at junctions, the air always faintly scented with coal smoke, leather, and hope.

During the day, she drifted from car to car when she could, stretching her legs, trading jokes with strangers who looked as nervous as she felt. At night, she tried to sleep sitting up, her neck complaining and her nerves humming.

She had stayed in two boardinghouses so far when the train stopped overnight—one with lumpy mattresses and watery soup, another with a landlady who spoke as though everyone owed her an apology.

"Lord," Belle had whispered in that second boardinghouse, staring up at a ceiling stained by rain and time, "if this is a sample of what's ahead, I promise I will not complain about my mama's lumpy pillows ever again. Please bless this mattress. It feels like I'm sleeping on a sack of disgruntled potatoes."

She could not see the road ahead, but she could feel it. The further west they went, the less familiar the landscape became. Trees thinned. Fields widened. It looked as if God had taken the world and stretched it like dough, leaving a great, flat expanse where anything could happen.

"Seven more days," she told herself each morning. "Seven more days and I'll be where I'm meant to be."

A Quiet Car and a Simple Prayer

On the day the sky changed, she was in the last car.

The train had taken on new passengers at a junction town whose name she barely caught—something with "Creek" or "Grove" in it. The platform had been crowded, the air full of shouts and steam, mothers scolding children, conductors waving flags.

Belle, tired of noise and eager to be alone with her thoughts, had slipped back through the cars until she reached the final one. It was sparsely occupied, mostly crates and trunks, with a few scattered seats bolted to the floor.

"Perfect," she murmured. "Just me, my thoughts, and my attempts not to worry myself into foolishness."

She took a seat near the back door, where a small, smudged window gave her a view of the tracks unspooling behind them like a dark ribbon. Her doctor's bag rested on the floor by her ankle, solid and reassuring.

She folded her hands in her lap.

"All right, Lord," she whispered, "it's just You and me back here. I thought maybe we could have a little talk before I start bothering You about food again."

The rhythm of the train soothed her, the steady clack-clack-clack like a heartbeat.

"I know You know where this train is going," she said quietly. "I know You know where I'm supposed to end up. I'm trying my best to trust You. You might have noticed that I still get nervous. Especially at night. Especially when I start thinking of all the things that could go wrong and all the people I haven't met yet who might be depending on me not to faint over a little blood."

She smiled faintly, even as she spoke.

"So I wanted to say thank You," she went on. "Thank You for getting me this far. For keeping the wheels on and the boiler from exploding, and for not letting anybody's chicken escape from their crate and peck my ankles. I appreciate the details, even if I forget to say so."

Her smile faded a little.

"And… if I'm honest—since You already know—I'm scared. I don't know the people I'm going to serve. I don't know if they'll listen. I don't know if they'll laugh at my size or my accent or my ideas. But You do. And as long as You'll walk with me, I'll keep walking."

The train rattled on. She closed her eyes.

"Also," she added, "if You see fit to keep storms far from the tracks, I'd be much obliged."

The Sky Changes

It happened so quickly that later Belle would struggle to put it into words.

One moment, the sky outside the small window was ordinary—pale, with streaks of cloud dragging behind them. The land rolled gently away on either side, empty but not unfriendly.

The next moment, the light dimmed.

It wasn't the slow darkening of evening, nor the brief blotting of a cloud passing the sun. It was as if someone had taken a thick gray curtain and pulled it straight across the heavens.

Belle opened her eyes and frowned, turning to look fully out the glass. The air outside seemed heavy, thick, wrong.

"What in the…?"

She rose, bracing herself as the train swayed. Something in her chest tightened, a prickle along her spine. She knew weather. She knew storms. She'd seen thunderheads roll over the farm like armies on the march.

This was different.

The wind picked up, buffeting the side of the car. The metal walls creaked in protest. Far ahead, she heard the faint, frantic blow of the train's whistle, long and urgent.

The hair on her arms stood on end.

"Oh no," she breathed. "No, no, no…"

27

She moved closer to the back door, pressing her palms to the glass. The clouds were not just dark—they were twisting, folding in on themselves. A funnel formed in the distance, long and pale against the bruised sky, reaching from heaven to earth like a finger of terrible intent.

A tornado.

Her heart slammed against her ribs.

"Lord," she whispered, breath coming fast, "I know I said I didn't want storms near the tracks. I feel like this is the opposite of that."

The funnel danced, jittering, then steadied, growing larger, closer. The wind screamed. The train shuddered.

Someone shouted in the car ahead of her. The sound was snatched away by the roar of the storm.

Lifted

The world lurched.

Belle grabbed for the nearest seatback, her fingers sliding on polished wood. The last car bucked like a horse, thrown sideways by a force too strong to be ignored.

There was a horrible, tearing sound—a wrenching, grinding shriek of metal parting from metal.

The coupling.

Her stomach dropped as the last car wrenched free of the train.

For a heartbeat—one impossible, suspended heartbeat—there was a strange, weightless sensation. The clatter of wheels on rails ceased. Noise turned to thunder, then to something beyond sound, a roaring that seemed to come from everywhere at once.

The car lifted.

It did not feel like rising so much as being seized.

Belle was thrown sideways, then up, then sideways again. She slammed into a seat, her shoulder exploding with pain. Her doctor's bag flew from the floor and landed squarely on her chest, driving the breath from her lungs.

She tried to cry out. Air refused to cooperate.

The car spun, twisted—she could not tell which way was up. Window glass shattered, flying like cruel rain. Wood splintered. Metal groaned. The world became a mad whirl of color and pain and movement.

In the center of that chaos, Belle did the only thing her spirit knew how to do.

She prayed.

The words that came were not the careful, measured phrases she used in church or the polite requests she spoke before meals. They came from deep inside, from a place where fear and faith collided. A rush of syllables, her prayer language pouring out of her like water breaking a dam.

Her lips moved even as she could not hear herself over the roar.

"Jesus, Jesus, Jesus..." she gasped between the flood of unformed words. "I'm Yours. I'm Yours. I'm Yours..."

The car spun.

Time unraveled, stretched, snapped.

She had no idea how long she was in the grip of the storm. It could have been seconds. It felt like forever. The car was no longer moving forward on tracks—it was whirling in some terrible dance, caught in the eye of a power she could neither fight nor understand.

All she could do was cling to the bag pressed against her chest and to the Name she knew by heart.

The Landing

The impact, when it came, was sudden.

The car dropped—she felt it—and then slammed into the earth with a bone-rattling crash. Wood shrieked. Glass cracked. Something heavy fell nearby with a dull thud.

Belle was thrown forward and then backward, her head snapping hard against the cushioned back of a bolted seat. Stars burst behind her eyes. The world snapped to black for a moment, then wavered back into hazy, spinning focus.

Silence followed.

Not the silence of peace, but the stunned hush that comes when violence pauses to see what it has done.

Her ears rang. Every inch of her body ached. Her chest rose and fell in shallow, desperate breaths beneath the weight of her doctor's bag.

"I… am… still… here," she croaked.

Her own voice sounded strange, far away.

She tried to move her fingers. They twitched.

She tried to wiggle her toes. They obeyed, though they protested.

She drew in a deeper breath, winced at a streak of pain along her ribs, and then slowly, carefully, lifted the bag off her chest. Bruises screamed their displeasure but held.

"Thank You," she whispered. "Oh, Lord, thank You. I don't know what You just did, but I'm still breathing, and I'd very much like to keep it that way."

The car felt… wrong. Tilted. She realized she was half-lying, half-sitting at an angle. The seats around her were twisted. One bench hung at an impossible slant, bolts ripped from the floor. Sunlight slanted in at odd angles through shattered windows and torn boards.

She turned her head—slowly, carefully. No one else was there.

Of all the things that could have happened in that spinning madness, the car had emptied itself of everyone but her at some point. Or she had been the only one to wander back hereat the last car. Either way, she was alone.

"Of course," she muttered, grimacing as she tried to sit up. "The one time I'm in a wreck, I don't even have someone to complain to about it."

Her humor was a thin shield, but it was still a shield.

She braced her feet and pushed, using the back of the seat as leverage. Her body protested, but strength answered. Bit by bit, she pulled herself upright.

Dizziness washed over her. The room—no, the car— tilted, spun. She closed her eyes and took slow breaths.

31

"In," she muttered. "Out. You've delivered calves that fought harder than this, Annabelle. Don't you dare faint now."

When the spinning eased, she opened her eyes again.

The back door, which had been solidly shut before, was now warped and half-cracked, the metal frame twisted as if some giant hand had tried to wrinkle it like paper. Glass littered the floor in jagged, glittering patches. One side of the car had bowed outward. The other side was half-buried in earth.

She had landed.

Where, she had no idea.

Opening the Way

She needed to get out.

That much was clear.

Belle slung the strap of her doctor's bag across her chest. The familiar weight steadied her. She picked her way carefully over shattered glass and bent metal, boots crunching on debris. A loose pipe dangled from the ceiling. She ducked under it, muttering, "Don't you dare fall on me, I have enough bruises."

The back door was jammed. It hung crookedly in its frame, gaps where light filtered through in thin spears.

She set her jaw.

"Lord," she whispered, "You got me through a tornado. Please don't let me be defeated by a door."

She tested it first with her hands, pushing, pulling, feeling where it gave and where it held. The upper hinge had torn loose; the lower still clung stubbornly.

"Of course," she said under her breath. "There's always one hinge that won't mind."

She turned sideways and drove her shoulder into the door with a grunt. Pain flared fresh in muscles already battered. The metal groaned.

Again.

"Come on," she gasped. "Open up. In the name of Jesus, I am not staying in this box."

She threw herself against it a third time, adding a prayer in her prayer language to the force of her body. Something snapped—the protesting shriek of metal giving way.

The door lurched outward, then sagged, hanging at a new, more generous angle.

A breeze slipped in.

Belle leaned her forehead against the cool edge of the doorframe for a moment, breathing hard.

"Thank You," she whispered. "I mean it. Thank You."

Then she squeezed through the space, boots sliding down the crumpled outer step, and dropped onto solid ground.

The Field

She straightened slowly, one hand resting on the side of the overturned car.

The sky above her was blue.

Not the bruised, swirling chaos of moments ago, but the kind of clear, crisp blue that made her think of fresh-washed laundry hung on a line. A few small clouds drifted lazily, as if nothing in the world had ever been wrong.

The train was gone.

So were the tracks.

The car she had just escaped from lay at a drunken angle in what looked like the middle of nowhere. No station. No town. No trees. Just an open expanse of land that stretched in every direction—flat and wide and empty.

"Well," Belle said aloud, because silence felt too big, "this is not on the schedule."

She turned in a slow circle.

Nothing.

No smoke in the distance. No fences. No houses. No line of rails gleaming toward some known destination.

A desolate field, that was all. Grass flattened in some places by the violence of the car's landing, standing tall and indifferent in others. The silence was so complete it hummed.

She swallowed.

"All right," she said, her voice sounding small in the open air. "All right, Annabelle Foster, you are not dead. That's the good news. The bad news is… everything else."

She adjusted the strap of her bag on her shoulder.

"Lord," she said, gazing up at the deceptively innocent sky, "I do not pretend to understand Your travel plans. But I'm going to keep talking to You as if this is not the worst idea I've ever been part of."

Her legs felt shaky, but they held. She took a tentative step, then another.

The ground was solid beneath her boots, a mixture of packed earth and stubborn grass. No mud, no rocks to twist an ankle on, no obvious holes to fall into. Just emptiness.

She looked back at the wrecked car.

"I suppose I should be glad I'm not still in you," she told it. "But if you had any sense of direction to share before I leave, now would be the time."

It said nothing, which she took as rude but understandable.

Walking and Praying

She picked a direction.

There was no particular logic to it—just a sense that if she stood still too long, fear would cement her to the spot. So she chose the direction where the horizon looked ever so slightly less monotonous, hoisted her bag more securely, and began to walk.

Each step jarred her bruises. Her ribs ached. Her shoulder throbbed. A dull, insistent pounding had taken up residence at the base of her skull.

"I am going to feel this tomorrow," she muttered. "Assuming I am alive and not part of some eternal field-walking exercise by then."

35

The air was cooler than it had been inside the car. A faint breeze brushed her face, carrying the faint scent of dry grass and dust. No smoke, no food, no people.

"Lord," she said after a few minutes, "I'm going to talk out loud so I don't start screaming. I know You don't need volume to hear me, but I need it to remember I'm still here."

Her voice steadied her.

"I'm scared," she admitted. "I know You know that, but I need to say it. My stomach feels like someone tied it in a knot, and my knees are not impressed with this situation. I don't know where I am. I don't know which way the train went. I don't know if anyone even knows that this car is missing."

She laughed, a short, breathless sound.

"On the bright side," she added, "I'm fairly certain no one else is using this field at the moment, so privacy is not an issue."

Her humor wobbled, but it was still there.

The sun climbed slowly higher. Time blurred. Without landmarks, minutes and miles tangled.

"How far did we go, anyway?" she wondered aloud. "How far can a tornado toss a whole train car? Mills and miles? Probably more than I want to think about."

A sudden pang of worry struck her.

"What about the rest of the train?" she whispered. "Lord, please… please let them be all right. If You spared me here, I can't bear the thought of everyone else…" She couldn't finish the sentence. "Just—cover them. Wherever they are. Please."

The field went on.

She kept walking.

"One step," she told herself. "Then another. You've walked cow pastures more confusing than this. At least here nothing has tried to eat your hem yet."

Strange Sounds

After what felt like an hour—though it might have been less, or more—she began to hear something besides her own footsteps and her own muttering.

At first it was faint. A sound carried on the wind, rising and falling, difficult to place.

She stopped, head tilted.

"There now," she murmured. "What are you?"

It came again—a call, then another. Not human voices, exactly, but not entirely like the calls of animals she knew either. It was as if the land itself were… speaking.

A prickling ran down her arms.

"Lovely," she said under her breath. "Either I'm hearing things, or the local wildlife has learned to sing."

She took a cautious step forward, then another.

The calls grew a little stronger as she moved: high notes, low notes, something that might have been a whoop or a chant, or both. She could not tell if it was coming from ahead of her, to the side, or some shifting point between.

"Lord," she whispered, "I am not opposed to meeting new neighbors. I would simply prefer they be the kind that don't eat lost doctors."

A gust of wind carried the sound more clearly—a rise and fall, rhythmic. Almost like… signals.

She swallowed, pulse quickening.

"Animals?" she asked aloud. "People? Both? Neither?"

Her mind offered possibilities she did not particularly enjoy: wild horses, coyotes, wolves, or something less familiar. Or perhaps it was a group of people, ones who knew this land far better than she did, calling to one another across the emptiness.

Her heart thudded faster.

"Lord," she said, "You know I want to help people in the West. I did not specify how You were going to introduce us. If this is the beginning of that introduction, I would appreciate it if You'd keep my head attached and my limbs unchewed."

The sounds came again, a little closer, a little clearer. She still could not parse them, but there was a pattern— rises and falls, pauses, repeats.

She wiped her palms on her skirt.

"All right," she breathed. "Whatever this is, I can't stand here forever. Either I walk toward it, or it walks toward me. And if I'm going to be found, I'd rather be the one praying upright than curled in a ball sobbing."

She adjusted her grip on the bag's strap, straightened her sore shoulders, and resumed walking, one careful step at a time.

"Lord," she whispered, "You got me through the storm. Don't leave me now in the quiet."The field stretched ahead—wide, empty, humming with unseen life.

The strange calls rose on the wind again.

Belle kept walking.

CHAPTER FOUR

Found in the Quiet

Belle did not collapse with any dignity at all.

There was no dramatic stagger. No heroic last step. No final prayer shouted toward heaven in poetic surrender.

She simply stopped.

Her knees buckled as if they had reached a unanimous decision without consulting the rest of her, and down she went—right into the stubborn grass, doctor's bag thumping beside her like an accusation.

"Well," she muttered faintly, cheek pressed against the earth, "this is… unfortunate."

The sun had shifted higher while she walked, turning generous warmth into something sharp and insistent. Her tongue felt thick in her mouth. Her thoughts slowed, dragging like boots through mud. She had tried to ration her energy, tried to keep walking with purpose instead of panic, but purpose did not replace water.

Her last coherent thought was vaguely irritated.

"Lord," she whispered, so quietly she wasn't sure the words made it past her lips, "I would prefer not to die in a field like a misplaced turnip."

Then the world slid sideways.

Water

Cold.

That was the first thing she noticed.

Not the comforting cool of shade, but the shocking splash of something poured with intent. It struck her cheek, ran into her hair, soaked the collar of her dress.

She sputtered.

"All right," she croaked, eyes still shut, "I'm awake. You can stop trying to drown me now."

A murmur rose around her—voices, low and startled.

She frowned.

That didn't sound like angels.

She blinked, squinting, forcing her eyes open.

The world resolved slowly.

Canvas above her. Slanted poles. Shadows dancing in firelight. The air thick with the scent of smoke, herbs, and cooked grain.

She was lying on blankets.

Her head snapped to the side—too fast—and she groaned, clutching her temples.

"Ohhh… I officially retract all previous complaints," she muttered. "This is worse."

A woman knelt beside her, dark hair braided close, eyes sharp but not unkind. She held a small cup and tipped it carefully again.

"Drink," the woman said, her English accented but clear. "Slow."

Belle froze.

English.

She took a careful sip, then another. Cool water slid down her throat, blessed and miraculous.

"Thank You, Jesus," Belle breathed, tears springing to her eyes without permission.

A man crouched nearby, tall, lean, his expression unreadable. He said something to the woman in a language Belle did not know—soft but deliberate.

Belle swallowed again, her heart picking up pace.

"Oh," she said faintly. "Oh no."

The shapes around her sharpened as awareness returned. Men. Women. Children. All watching. All still.

A Native village.

Or at least… what remained of one.

"Okay," Belle said carefully, every instinct screaming at her to stay calm, stay respectful, and not faint again. "Before anyone panics—or sacrifices me, or whatever the plan is—please know I'm very grateful to be alive. Also very tired."

The woman's lips twitched.

"You speak much," she said.

"Yes," Belle admitted. "It's how I cope."

A ripple of something passed through the gathered faces. Not laughter—not yet—but curiosity.

Belle took a slow breath.

"My name is Annabelle Foster," she said, then paused. "But Belle is fine. I answer to both."

She glanced around the teepee, then back at the woman with the water.

"And you are…?"

The woman hesitated, then said, "My name is Sahkîwēw." She tapped her chest. "That means river light."

Belle nodded solemnly. "That's a beautiful name. Mine means 'grace.' I would like to live up to it today."

This time, there was a soft chuckle—unmistakably laughter.

"How did I get here?"

A man stepped forward then, older, his hair streaked with gray. He leaned on a carved staff, eyes studying her not as prey, not as threat—but as a puzzle.

"You walked into the heat," he said. His voice was calm. Authority without cruelty. "You prayed while you walked."

Belle stiffened.

"I did?" she asked.

"You did," he confirmed. "Out loud."

She winced. "Of course I did."

He went on. "We saw you before you saw us. For many hours."

Belle's eyes widened.

"You followed me?"

43

The woman—Sahkîwēw—nodded. "You were walking toward our people. Toward sickness."

Belle exhaled slowly. "That sounds about right."

The man gestured gently. "You fell. The sun took you. We did not let it finish."

She stared at him, then around again, piecing things together.

"How," she asked slowly, "did you move me?"

This, evidently, pleased them.

Several women smiled outright now. A younger man snorted and turned away, shoulders shaking.

Sahkîwēw folded her arms.

"You are heavy," she said simply.

Belle burst out laughing.

"Yes," she agreed fervently. "That is something I've been made aware of on many occasions."

The elder continued, unfazed. "We did not move you easily. Four men. Two women. The earth helped."

Belle pressed her lips together.

"I would like to apologize in advance to everyone's back."

Another ripple—real laughter now.

The tension shifted.

The Twisted Car

"You came from the sky," Sahkîwēw said.

Belle blinked. "I… beg your pardon?"

The elder nodded. "The iron beast screamed. The wind broke it. One part fell. Twisted."

Belle's heart thudded.

"The train car," she whispered.

"Yes," he said. "We found it. Empty."

Belle swallowed hard. "I was inside."

He studied her face closely. "The wind chose you."

"Well," Belle said weakly, "the wind and I have very different standards of adventure."

A younger woman spoke then, gesturing toward a pile near the entrance of the teepee.

"Your bag," she said. "We saw it before we saw you."

Belle turned her head.

Her doctor's bag sat there—dirty, scuffed, but unmistakable.

Relief flooded her so fast she had to blink.

"Oh thank God," she breathed. "I thought I'd lost that too."

The elder crouched, opened it carefully, and gestured to its contents.

"We know tools," he said. "We know healers. Your things speak."

Belle pushed herself up on her elbows, ignoring the protest of her muscles.

45

"I am a doctor," she said quietly. "And a cook. And currently—very, very lost."

There was a pause.

Then Sahkîwēw said softly, "We have sick."

The Signals

"How long," Belle asked slowly, "were you following me?"

The elder exchanged a glance with another man, then answered.

"Since you walked away from the iron shell. We sent voices."

Realization dawned.

"The sounds," Belle whispered. "The calls."

Sahkîwēw inclined her head. "You heard them."

"I heard them," Belle confirmed. "I just didn't know if they wanted to eat me."

The younger man laughed outright at that.

"No," he said. "Not eat."

"Good," Belle nodded. "Because I don't think I'd sit well."

More laughter.

The elder continued. "We are not settled. We are moving."

Belle's brow furrowed.

"Moving… how?"

His gaze turned distant. "We walk where we are told. Sometimes we rest. Sometimes sickness follows. Sometimes babies come when bodies are too tired."

Her chest tightened.

"The trail," she whispered.

He did not confirm it aloud—but his silence did.

Belle closed her eyes briefly.

"Oh," she said softly. "Oh Lord."

Food, Then almost darkenss

Someone pressed a wooden bowl into her hands. Warm. Thick stew. Roots, herbs, something hearty.

"Eat," Sahkîwēw urged. "You live better if you eat."

Belle did not argue. She took small bites, mindful of her stomach, but hunger roared too loudly to ignore.

"This," she said faintly, after a few mouthfuls, "is very good."

Sahkîwēw allowed herself a proud smile. "Food keeps people here."

The elder watched Belle closely as she ate.

"After we brought you," he said, "you spoke words we did not know. Soft. Fast. Many."

Belle froze, spoon halfway to her mouth.

"I… did?"

"Yes," he said. "In sleep."

She swallowed.

47

"I was praying," she said simply.

He nodded, as if that settled something important.

Her vision wavered.

"Oh," she murmured. "I think…"

The bowl tipped slightly in her hands.

Sahkîwēw reached for it just in time as Belle slumped back onto the blankets.

"Too soon," Belle muttered, eyelids fluttering. "Doctor's orders—rest."

And then—

Darkness, again.

This time, gentler.

Watched Over

As Belle slept, the elder straightened.

"She stays," he said.

Sahkîwēw nodded. "She heals."

One of the younger men frowned. "She is white."

"She is also wounded," the elder replied. "And alive."

Outside, the wind passed through the grass like a held breath released.

Inside, Annabelle Foster slept—bruised, dehydrated, confused, and still breathing.

Her story had not ended in the field.

It had just taken another turn.

CHAPTER FIVE

When the Healer Was Healed

For three days, Annabelle Foster did not rise.

This troubled her deeply at first.

The woman who had crossed states, endured storms, walked for hours beneath a brutal sun, and survived being tossed from the sky by a tornado did not appreciate being humbled by something as ordinary as her own body's collapse.

On the first day, she kept trying to sit up.

On the second day, she stopped trying and started negotiating with the Lord.

By the third day, she surrendered entirely.

Her world narrowed to the canvas roof above her, the hush of movement beyond the teepee walls, and the slow rhythm of breath returning where it had nearly fled.

Her head throbbed dully. Her muscles felt bruised clear to the bone. When she attempted to move too quickly, the world tilted sideways as if reminding her that strength was not presently hers to command.

"Well," she whispered hoarsely on the second morning, staring at the shadows overhead, "this is not how I pictured being useful."

A soft chuckle answered her—hers.

"You always do this," she said quietly to herself. "You rush ahead and call it obedience."

She closed her eyes and let the sound of her own breathing anchor her.

When words failed her—when English felt too rigid to hold what stirred inside—her prayer language rose instead. Not loudly. Not for show. Just a soft, steady murmur beneath her breath, flowing like water over stones.

She praised God without lifting her head.

She thanked Him for life.
She thanked Him for water.
She thanked Him for strangers who chose mercy.

Sometimes the prayers slipped into praise songs half-remembered from childhood. Sometimes they were wordless sounds formed by trust rather than thought.

She did not know who might hear her.

She did not care.

The Sounds of a People in Pain

While Belle lay still, the life of the camp moved around her.

She heard crying—sharp, sudden wails that cut through the air like torn fabric. She heard children's footsteps running past the tent, light and fast, carrying urgency. She heard older voices calling out in rhythms she did not understand.

More than once she tried to push herself up, heart tugging toward the sound.

"Not yet," her body insisted.

Twice a day they fed her.

Simple food. Broth. Soft grains. Warm roots pounded smooth. Someone lifted the bowl to her lips when her hands shook too much.

She did not argue.

Once, embarrassment flared when they brought her a bedpan.

"Oh," she muttered weakly, cheeks warming, "I had hoped we were better acquainted before it came to this."

The woman assisting her did not so much as blink.

"You are alive," she said plainly. "That is enough."

Cold cloths were laid across Belle's forehead when her skin burned. Hands steady and practiced checked her pulse. Someone whispered near her ear when restlessness took her late at night.

"You stay."

She slept. She woke. She prayed.

Something inside her loosened.

A Turning of the Heart

On the third night, as the moonlight filtered faintly through the canvas, Belle found herself crying—not from pain, but from clarity.

"I see it now," she whispered to Jesus. "I wanted to serve You strong. Capable. Certain. I didn't want to need anyone."

Her voice trembled.

"But You waited until I was still. Until I had nothing left to prove."

Tears slid into her hair.

"I thought losing everything meant failure. But You stripped it away so I would finally listen."

She took a slow, trembling breath.

"I don't have my medicines. I don't have my tools. I don't even have my dignity half the time." A ghost of a laugh escaped her. "All I have left is You."

Peace came—not loud, not dramatic, but sure.

Stillness became obedience.

The Cry That Changed Everything

On the fourth day, Belle sat up.

Not gracefully.

More like a determined collection of groans, careful bracing, and stubborn willpower.

"There," she whispered triumphantly. "Vertical."

The world swayed but did not betray her.

Moments later, a cry split the air.

Not the sharp, startled cry of fear—but the deep, raw, unmistakable sound of a woman in labor.

Belle froze.

Something shifted.

Pain. Fear. Muscle memory.

Her spine straightened.

Her mind sharpened.

She knew that sound.

She swung her legs over the edge of the bedding.

"Oh," she breathed. "Oh no. No no no."

The cry came again—longer this time. Desperate.

Belle's heart leapt into her throat.

"Lord," she whispered urgently, "I am not ready."

Silence answered.

Then resolve.

She pushed herself upright and staggered out of the tent.

The Doctor Awakens

Inside another shelter, the air was thick with urgency.

A woman lay on piled blankets, her face pale and slick with sweat. Her breathing came in short gasps. Other women hovered nearby, fear etched into their features.

The moment Belle crossed the threshold, instinct took over.

"Move," she said—not unkindly, but firmly.

They did.

She knelt beside the laboring woman, hands steady now, eyes sharp.

"How long?" Belle asked.

Hands gestured. Words tumbled in fragments. Time stretched backward and forward all at once.

Belle examined carefully.

Her breath caught.

"Breach," she whispered.

She swallowed hard and straightened.

"Soap," she said clearly. "Clean cloths. Boiling water."

They hesitated only a moment, then moved.

Belle closed her eyes briefly.

"Jesus," she whispered, forehead dropping to the woman's leg, "I know what to do, and I don't know what to do. Please don't let me stand here alone."

The mother cried out again—weak now. Exhausted.

Belle positioned herself with professional calm, ignoring the ache in her limbs.

"All right," she murmured. "All right, sweetheart. I'm right here."

She worked carefully. Slowly.

But the baby would not turn.

Minutes passed like hours.

Fear crept cold along Belle's spine.

She placed her hands gently on the woman's swollen belly and prayed.

Out loud.

"Jesus, this baby belongs to You. This mother belongs to You. I have done all I know to do. If You do not intervene, they will die."

Silence pressed in.

Belle tried again—more carefully, more deliberately.

This time—

She felt it.

Not resistance.

Guidance.

A warmth.

A steadiness beyond muscle and bone.

Her hands moved with a confidence that was not her own.

"Oh," she whispered, breath hitching. "Oh, You're here."

She guided the baby again.

The position changed.

The head turned.

"Push," Belle urged gently. "Now—push."

The woman cried out.

"Push again!"

The baby came.

A thin, sharp wail pierced the shelter.

Belle laughed and sobbed at once.

"There you are," she whispered. "There you are."

The mother collapsed back, weak but breathing.

"She will live," Belle said quietly. "Both will."

A holy hush fell.

The Beginning of Months

That night, Belle collapsed back into her bedding—shaking, exhausted, transformed.

She whispered into the darkness.

"You did that," she told Jesus. "You did all of it."

From that night on, she stayed.

She traveled as they traveled. She rested when they rested. She listened. She learned.

Without medicine, she learned herbs. Without instruments, she learned hands. Without certainty, she learned surrender.

Before every case, she spoke to Jesus.

Before every birth, every fever, every wound, she asked—not with fear, but trust.

And miracles followed.

Not every time.

But enough.

Enough that hope returned.

Enough that questions were asked.

Enough that Belle, once lost, now stood fully in her calling.

"Tell me about your Jesus," a woman asked one night.

Belle smiled softly.

“I'd love to.”

And she began.

CHAPTER SIX

When Staying Would Cost Too Much

Belle first sensed the trouble before anyone spoke her name.

It was the quiet that shifted—not the peaceful stillness she had come to know, but a different kind, one that bristled and watched its own shadow. Conversations paused when she passed. Men who usually greeted her with nods held their mouths tight. Fires burned lower at night, though the air had grown no colder.

News had arrived.

She learned this while cleaning her instruments near the edge of camp, her doctor's bag open beside her as she wiped steel that had already been cleaned twice before. She did this when she was thinking too hard—found order where she could, even if the world insisted on disorder.

A young man approached her slowly, boots careful against the ground.

"You should come to the fire," he said quietly.

Belle looked up. "Is someone sick?"

He hesitated. "Not the way you fix."

Her chest tightened.

She closed the bag and followed.

The News from the Trading Post

The men had returned that morning from the trading post along the trail. They sat together now, faces drawn, hands wrapped around cups that had long since gone cold.

One of them spoke first.

"The white men were there."

Belle stopped walking.

She had known, of course. She had always known this day would come. Still, knowing something in your spirit did not keep your heart from racing when it arrived.

"They asked questions," another continued. "About a woman taken by the storm."

Belle crossed her arms lightly, grounding herself.

"They described me," she said, not asking.

"Yes," the man replied. "Your hair. Your build. A woman who traveled alone. A woman who vanished."

A breath passed through Belle's lips.

"Did they say why?" she asked.

"They said she must be returned," the man answered. "That they would send Texas Rangers if necessary."

That did it.

A low murmur rippled through the group—anger, fear, old scars reopening all at once.

Texas Rangers.

Belle had never met one, but she knew what their arrival meant in places already burdened by enough eyes and expectations.

59

She lifted her chin.

"I never wanted to bring trouble here," she said quietly.

The elder stepped forward.

"We know," he said simply. "That is why this is hard."

Division in the Camp

That evening, the arguments began.

Not shouting, not cruelty—but worry sharpened into edges that cut anyway.

"If she stays, they will come," one voice insisted.
"They hunt us whether she is here or not," another snapped.
"She saves lives," a woman cried.
"She brings eyes," a man countered.

Belle listened from the shadows, unseen but not unaware.

Her heart pulled in opposite directions.

She wanted to shout, Let me decide.
She wanted to beg, Please let me stay.
She wanted to disappear so no one would have to choose.

None of those were answers.

Finally, the elder raised his staff.

"She is not an object to be argued over," he said. "She is a woman with a calling. We will ask her what she desires—and we will listen."

All eyes turned toward Belle.

Belle Speaks

She stepped into the circle, hands clasped tightly to keep them from shaking.

"If you ask what I want," she said honestly, "I want to stay."

A murmur swept through the women.

She continued before courage deserted her.

"I want to keep healing. I want to walk with you. I want to learn from you. I want to serve God right where I am."

She paused, swallowing.

"But I will not stay if it means men with guns and papers come looking for me and decide you are the problem."

Her voice cracked despite her best effort.

"I will not repay mercy with danger."

Silence followed.

Finally, the elder spoke.

"What does your Jesus say?"

Belle's breath caught.

"I don't know yet," she admitted. "But I will ask Him."

Waiting for the Answer

Waiting was harder than storms.

Belle prayed constantly during those days—but not desperately. Not fearfully. She had learned better.

At night, she walked to the edge of the camp, watching stars burn silently overhead.

"Lord," she whispered, "You taught me to stay when I wanted to run. Please don't ask me to run when I finally want to stay."

She thought about the people they passed on the trail.

Families moving in clusters—Black families traveling together for safety and dignity, bound by faith and determination.

Scottish families with wagons and worn Bibles, accents thick, hopes thicker.

Mexican families reclaiming soil through sweat and prayer.

Chinese families heading toward homestead allotments, walking quietly through suspicion and longing.

Everyone moving west.

Everyone seeking a place to belong.

And she—called somewhere specific before the storm ever came.

"I said yes," she whispered. "I don't want fear to rewrite my obedience."

God Answers Moving

God answered not with thunder, but wheels.

The sound came first—music carrying on the wind, laughter, the creak of wagons painted in rich colors, scarves fluttering like banners of defiance against dust.

A traveling Romani caravan approached.

The camp stirred.

"They need healing," someone told Belle softly. "Children. Elders."

Her heart leapt so hard it hurt.

She followed the pull before her mind could protest.

Another People in Need

The caravan welcomed her cautiously, eyes curious, hands open.

One man spoke for the group.

"We heard there was a healer among the people here," he said. "Is that you?"

"Yes," Belle replied. "If you will have me."

They had many needs.

A badly set arm. An infection carried too far. Exhausted mothers and worn-down elders.

Belle worked without hesitation—her instruments steady, her prayers constant, her confidence returning like muscle memory.

That night, around their fire, the man spoke again.

"We travel toward the homesteads," he said. "Toward the trading routes beyond."

Belle's breath left her in a rush.

"That is the direction of my assignment," she whispered.

The man smiled knowingly. "Then this is no accident."

"We will take you with us," he said.

Truth Settles In

When Belle returned to the Native camp, the elder was waiting.

"You have heard your answer," he said.

"Yes," she whispered.

"You will leave."

Tears rose quickly.

"I don't want to," she said. "I don't want to leave you."

He placed his palm against her forearm.

"If you stayed, they would come harder," he said gently. "And we already carry too much."

That truth settled deeper than grief.

The women gathered around Belle.

"We will miss you," one whispered.

"You walk in God's steps," another said.

Sahkîwēw held her face and pressed their foreheads together.

"You belong to the road," she said again.

Goodbye

Belle cried openly.

So did they.

Hands were held. Blessings spoken. Tears shared without shame.

"I love you," Belle said over and over, because there were no better words.

When she finally turned away, her chest felt torn open.

She did not look back again until she reached the edge of the field.

"Jesus," she whispered, voice breaking, "thank You for loving me through them."

Then she stepped toward the waiting wagons.

Toward obedience.

Toward the road that still called her.

CHAPTER SEVEN

A Name That Traveled Ahead of Her

Belle learned about her reputation the way most inconvenient truths arrive—
not all at once, not cruelly, but honestly.

It came during an evening fire, when the wagons had circled and the dust had settled into the hems of skirts and the cuffs of trousers. The air smelled of boiling roots and wood smoke, and someone had begun tuning a fiddle that clearly resented being hauled across half the territory.

Belle sat on an upturned crate, mending a tear in her skirt with practiced hands. The road had been kind to her body but unkind to her clothing.

A woman from the caravan—dark-haired, sharp-eyed, and impossibly calm—sat beside her.

"You know they speak of you ahead of us," the woman said casually.

Belle did not look up. "People usually do."

The woman smiled faintly. "This time, it is… complicated."

Belle tied off the thread and sighed. "All right. Tell me."

"They say a white woman traveled with the Native people. That she lived among them." The woman paused. "They say she prays strangely. That storms follow her, and healing too."

Belle winced. "Storms were not intentional."

"That you disappeared from proper society," the woman continued. "That you do not behave as respectable women should."

Belle chuckled despite herself. "That accusation is painfully accurate."

The woman turned, studying Belle's profile.

"They will not understand you," she said gently. "Especially the religious ones."

Belle's fingers stilled.

"They may shun you. Refuse you."

Belle nodded slowly. "That would not be new."

Friendly… or Not

Later that night, Belle lay beneath the stars, hands folded over her chest, eyes tracing constellations she half remembered from childhood.

"Friendliness," she whispered.

The Romani called it that. The way towns decided who belonged and who did not. The way smiles hardened into barriers when stories traveled faster than truth.

She had been friendly once.

She had been welcomed.

She remembered pews and hymns and women who smiled with their mouths but measured with their eyes.

She exhaled slowly.

"Jesus," she prayed, "I am going to need You to walk in rooms before I enter them. I cannot carry my own reputation."

She smiled faintly into the dark.

"I tried once. It went poorly."

People Who Knew the Price of Survival

The Romani did not speak of reputations lightly.

They knew them like weather.

They knew how a whisper could close a door before a foot crossed the threshold. They knew how labels fed children and starved dignity at the same time.

One night, while Belle cleaned her instruments by lantern light, a young man watched her curiously.

"You pray before you work," he said.

"Yes," Belle replied. "Before and sometimes during."

"And after," another added from nearby. "Especially after."

Belle smiled. "That too."

The woman who had spoken earlier—who earned money reading palms by day—sat cross-legged across from Belle.

"You know we do not believe the palms," she said matter-of-factly.

Belle raised an eyebrow. "That makes two of us."

"They expect it," the woman continued. "So we give them what they pay for. It buys food."

Belle nodded. "Survival is not faithlessness."

The woman studied her carefully. "Yet you pray. Always."

"Yes."

"And you believe."

"Yes."

"And the things that happen after…" She gestured vaguely, searching for the word. "They are not coincidence."

Belle set down her cloth.

"No," she said softly. "They're not."

When Questions Began

The questions came slowly at first.

Not challenges. Not debates.

Curiosity.

"Why do you talk to your God so openly?"
"Why do you ask instead of demand?"
"Why does your God heal some and not all?"

Belle answered what she could.

And when she did not know, she said so.

One evening, with the fire burning low, the palm reader asked gently, "Tell us who He is—your God."

Belle breathed in deeply.

"His name is Jesus," she said. "And He is not afraid of bad reputations."

They waited.

She continued, choosing her words with care, not polish.

"He was born of a virgin. Lived among working people. Traveled constantly. He touched the sick when others crossed the road to avoid them."

Someone snorted softly. "Sounds familiar."

"He was accused of keeping bad company," Belle said with a smile. "Which He did. On purpose."

They laughed.

"He healed, not to show power," Belle went on, "but to show love. And when people tried to make Him a king, He walked away. And when people tried to kill Him—well…"

She paused.

"They did."

The fire crackled.

"But death didn't keep Him."

Silence followed—not uncomfortable, but attentive.

"He rose," Belle said simply. "And because He lives, I pray. Not because I deserve answers. But because He listens."

The palm reader's voice softened. "And the miracles?"

Belle looked down at her hands.

"I bring skill," she said. "I bring herbs. I bring tea. I bring knowledge."

She lifted her eyes.

"But when that is not enough, He steps in."

What She Did Not Say

She did not tell them how often she had failed.

She did not tell them how many prayers had gone unanswered.

She did not tell them about her fear—of towns, of churches, of being measured and discarded again.

She did not need to.

They knew something about being misunderstood.

Shared Ground

Over the next days, they watched more closely.

They saw Belle sit with the sick long after exhaustion pressed against her spine.

They saw her whisper prayers no one prompted.

They saw her treat wounds with herbs when the instruments could do no more.

They saw fevers break.

Pain ease.

Children laugh again.

And when nothing happened—when death came anyway—they saw her mourn honestly.

One night, the young man spoke again.

"If your God is so powerful," he asked carefully, "why did He let people hate Him?"

Belle smiled sadly.

"Because love does not force itself," she said. "And people often fear what reminds them they could change."

The palm reader nodded slowly. "We know this God," she said. "Maybe not His name—but His way."

Belle's throat tightened.

"He knows you," she whispered.

Approaching Civilization

The sound of the railroad came before they saw it.

The distant whistle echoed across the land—a reminder that the moving world of rails and schedules and judgments lay ahead.

The wagons slowed.

Belle felt it like a tightening in her chest.

"Towns are near," someone said.

She swallowed.

Her reputation waited there.

The judgments.

The glances.

The doors that might close—or open.

She sat alone that night, stars fading as dawn approached, and prayed one final prayer before sleep.

"Jesus," she whispered, "I do not need to be understood. I need to be faithful."

She paused.

"But if You would soften the hearts of the friendly… I would be grateful."

The whistle blew again—closer this time.

Belle folded her hands, steady at last.

Whatever came next, she would not walk alone.

CHAPTER EIGHT

The Platform Between Worlds

The railroad station rose from the plain like a promise that had learned how to wait.

It was not large—just a wooden platform, a low building with peeling paint, and a single bench warped by years of weather and weary travelers. The tracks cut through the land like a stitched seam, one iron line pulling the world forward whether it was ready or not.

Belle stood a little apart at first, her doctor's bag resting by her side, the late afternoon sun catching the metal clasps. The sounds of the station surrounded her: the murmur of voices, the hiss of steam somewhere far down the line, the impatient shuffle of feet.

This place felt different from the camps.

This place felt like judgment wore a uniform.

The Romani women gathered around her, speaking softly among themselves as they counted coins—few, worn smooth, held tightly as though they might vanish if not respected.

One of them placed the small stack into Belle's hands.

"For the ticket," she said. "And food."

Belle stared at the money as if it were something sacred.

"I can't take this," she said immediately. "You need it."

The woman smiled sadly. "We will read more palms."

Belle winced. "You don't even believe in them."

"We believe in feeding our families," another woman replied simply. "And now… we believe in something else too."

That hit her harder than any storm.

Another woman stepped forward, holding Belle's hands firmly.

"We will buy a Bible," she said, eyes bright. "The Gospel of John. You said that is where we should start."

Belle's throat closed.

"Yes," she whispered. "That's a very good place."

They nodded solemnly, as if accepting a duty.

Waiting for the Train

They did not leave her.

Not one of them.

They waited there together—bright scarves and worn boots standing out among the drab station colors. Curious eyes followed them. A few mouths tightened disapprovingly. Belle felt it keenly now—the invisible line drawn between those who belonged and those who were merely passing through.

She prayed quietly.

"Lord, let kindness go ahead of me."

The train was late.

No one complained.

Instead, the Romani sat together on the ground near a small body of water just beyond the station—a shallow inlet where the land dipped gently.

They spoke in low voices.

Some laughed.

Some cried openly.

Belle realized suddenly just how much time had passed.

Almost two months.

Two months of shared meals, shared roads, shared questions about God and suffering and survival.

Two months of conversations that did not have to fit neatly into polite categories.

She knelt beside them as the sun began to dip.

"I'm going to miss our talks," she admitted, wiping her eyes. "You ask better questions than most churches."

One woman smiled wryly. "We have lived long enough to know lies when we hear them."

Another said softly, "And truth… when it stays."

Confessions at the Water

It happened quietly.

One by one.

No ceremony.

No witnesses from the station.

Just women stepping forward, eyes shining, voices trembling.

"I want Him," one said.

"I believe," another whispered.

"He hears me," a third breathed.

Belle's heart pounded.

"Do you understand what you're saying?" she asked gently. "He isn't a charm or protection from hardship."

They nodded.

"He stayed with us," one said simply.

Belle led them in the sinner's prayer—not rushed, not forced. She spoke of grace, forgiveness, new beginnings.

Tears fell freely.

Hands clasped.

When they finished, one woman glanced toward the water.

"Could you…?" she asked.

Belle's breath caught.

"Yes," she said. "If you want that."

They waded carefully into the shallow water, skirts gathered, laughter breaking through tears.

Belle baptized them one by one—hands steady, voice soft, authority quiet and sure.

"In the name of the Father, and the Son, and the Holy Spirit."

When they came out of the water, they hugged her fiercely, laughter and weeping tangled together.

"I don't know what my life looks like now," one woman said, "but I know Who walks with me."

Belle nodded, unable to speak.

The Dress

Before the whistle blew, they presented her with the dress.

It was beautiful—carefully sewn, richly colored, modest but striking. Something made for movement and dignity.

"For the train," they said.

"It's too much," Belle protested weakly.

"You will wear us with you," a woman replied. "So you don't forget."

As if she ever could.

Goodbye Again

The whistle sounded at last.

Sharp.

Final.

Time snapped back into order.

Belle hugged them again and again. Each goodbye felt like tearing cloth.

"I will carry you with me," she promised.

"And we will pray for you," they replied. "Even when people are unkind."

They watched as she boarded.

From the window, Belle looked down at them—colorful scarves bright against the gray station, hands raised, tears gleaming.

She pressed her palm to the glass.

"Jesus," she whispered, "thank You for loving me through them."

Four Days Away

The train lurched forward.

The platform shrank.

Another chapter closed behind her.

Her destination lay four days ahead.

Belle settled into her seat as night fell, exhaustion settling into her bones like grief.

She missed the Native camp.

Their quiet strength. Their herbal wisdom. Their fierce love for life and children.

She missed the Romani.

Their music. Their honesty. Their laughter that survived loss.

She did not understand why people built walls between such rich cultures.

The Native people had given her grounding, resilience, reverence for land and life.

The Romani had given her joy, adaptability, and fearless questions about faith.

Both had carried God in ways churches often forgot how to do.

"This world is poorer for its divisions," she murmured.

The train rocked gently as she leaned back, eyes closing.

The rhythmic clatter of the tracks lulled her into memory.

Faces drifted through her thoughts—smiles by firelight, hands clasped in prayer, children laughing, women brave enough to believe.

She felt the ache of goodbye settle deep and familiar.

"Lord," she whispered into the quiet car, "if this is the cost of obedience… let me never stop paying it with gratitude."

Outside the window, the land rolled on.

Inside, Belle rested—still breathing, still called, still learning that love always left marks on the faithful.

And the road, faithful as ever, carried her forward.

CHAPTER NINE

The Samaritan on the Platform

The train stopped the next morning in a town that barely seemed awake.

It was not meant to be a proper stop—just long enough to take on coal and water, long enough for a few passengers to step down and stretch stiff legs before being herded back aboard. The station was little more than a platform, a water tower, and a narrow street that led toward a cluster of buildings pretending to be civilization.

Belle watched from her seat as steam hissed and men shouted short commands. She had slept poorly, caught between memories of the Romani camp and the weight of what lay ahead. Her destination was still days away, but her heart already felt farther than that.

In the rear car, a small group of colored farmers and their families gathered their belongings—bundles tied with rope, baskets covered with cloth, children clutched close. They moved with quiet purpose.

Belle noticed them because they prayed out loud.

Not politely.

Not carefully.

They prayed the way people prayed who expected God to answer.

A woman near the aisle rocked gently, humming a tune that sounded like hope woven through sorrow. Two men spoke in low, rhythmic tones, their words tumbling into tongues that rose and fell like a tide.

Belle felt her chest loosen.

Finally, she thought. People who know how to pray without apology.

The porter, Abner Clay, moved through the car, calling out, "Fuel stop only! Anyone getting off, make it quick!"

He was a tall man with steady eyes and a presence that made chaos slow down when he entered a space.

The farming families began to rise—

And then someone cried out.

It was sudden. Sharp.

"He's down!"

An older man had collapsed near the door, his body folded awkwardly, his hat rolling away across the floor. His breathing came shallow, erratic.

Belle was on her feet before she thought.

Abner spun around. One look at the man on the floor, and then at Belle.

"Doctor?" he asked urgently.

Belle nodded. "Yes."

Abner didn't hesitate. He leaned down close to her.

"They won't treat him in this town," he said under his breath. "Local doctor don't see our people."

Belle's jaw tightened.

"We can take him to a hospital," she said.

Abner shook his head. "Nearest one that'll admit him is days away. Train won't wait."

Belle looked down at the man—gray-skinned now, sweat beading at his temples.

Her pulse steadied.

"Then I'm getting off the train," she said.

Abner grabbed her small valise and doctor's bag in one smooth motion.

"I thought you might," he said. "Come on."

The Platform Choice

The conductor shouted, "All aboard!"

Belle didn't look back.

She knelt beside the man as Abner and two others carefully lifted him onto a makeshift stretcher.

"Sir," Belle said firmly, pressing fingers to his wrist. "Can you hear me?"

The man's eyes flickered.

Belle glanced up. "What's his name?"

A woman stepped forward, tears running freely.

"This my husband," she said. "His name Elijah Turner."

Belle nodded. "All right, Mr. Turner. Stay with me."

The train whistle blew once. Then again.

Abner tightened his grip on Belle's bags.

"You know this train ain't waiting," he said.

"I know," Belle replied quietly. "I'll catch another."

The conductor frowned from the platform edge. "Miss, you getting back on or not?"

Belle didn't turn around.

"No," she said.

The train hissed and lurched forward.

Just like that, her seat rolled away from her.

Prayer That Moaned

They carried Elijah toward a large wagon waiting near the station—a sturdy thing, covered with canvas and already prepared for travel toward the nearby family farms.

Belle worked as they moved, loosening Elijah's collar, speaking steadily.

"Slow breaths," she instructed. "Slow. Stay with us."

The prayers rose around her—deep moans, groans that came from the belly, tongues spilling freely.

"Oh, Jesus…"
"Lord, don't take him…"
"Breathe life…"

Belle felt at home.

She pressed her palm firmly over Elijah's chest.

"Lord," she prayed aloud, unapologetic, "You see this man. You gave him breath. We're asking You to help him keep it."

Elijah gasped.

"Push that breath," Belle urged. "Don't give up."

To the Farm—or Not Yet

They set out toward the farms, wheels creaking over packed dirt. Some of the men stayed behind in town.

"Land office closes today," one explained grimly. "We gotta secure what we came for."

Belle nodded. Survival had many fronts.

She turned to the woman seated beside Elijah.

"Do you have medicines at home?" Belle asked gently.

The woman shook her head. "No ma'am."

Belle didn't pause.

"Let me off at the general store," she said. "Now."

The Store

The bell jingled sharply as Belle stepped inside.

The store went quiet.

A dozen pairs of eyes turned toward her—and then past her, to the wagon outside.

The storekeeper, a round man with a stiff collar and stiff ideas, frowned.

"What's your name?" he asked.

"Annabelle Foster," Belle replied calmly.

"And what exactly are you doing with… them?"

Belle smiled—not sweetly, but clearly.

"I'm a doctor," she said. "One of them had a heart attack on the train."

The man scoffed. "White women ain't doctors. And they sure ain't doctoring colored men."

The room tightened.

Belle laughed—once.

"Sir," she said pleasantly, "do you remember when Jesus spoke about the man beaten on the road?"

The man frowned. "What's that got to do with—"

"Only a Samaritan stopped to help," Belle continued. "Everyone else crossed the road."

She met his eyes evenly.

"I'm the Samaritan today."

Murmurs rippled through the shop.

A woman near the counter sniffed disapprovingly.

Belle turned back to the storekeeper.

"I need aspirin, alcohol, clean cloth, and whatever heart tonics you carry."

"And if I don't sell to you?"

Belle tilted her head.

"Then you get to explain to Jesus why you closed your door."

Silence.

Coins clinked onto the counter.

"Wrap them," Belle said.

Frowns and Faith

As Belle left, respectable townsfolk stared openly.

One woman whispered, "Shameful."

Belle whispered back, "Faithful."

She climbed back into the wagon, medicine in hand.

Elijah groaned weakly.

"I'm here," Belle told him. "You ain't done yet."

They prayed again—louder this time.

Moans turned into declarations.

Belle worked until sweat darkened her collar and her arms ached.

Hours passed.

At last, Elijah's breathing steadied.

The wagon rolled on.

That night, under unfamiliar stars, Belle sat beside the family fire.

She had no idea when she would catch the next train.

But she knew one thing for certain—

She was exactly where she was supposed to be.

End of Chapter Nine

Ms. Cherry, when you're ready, Chapter Ten can cover:

Life on the family farm

Town backlash

Belle's reputation spreading

Or the moment Texas Rangers do re-enter the story

Just tell me where to go next.

The Samaritan on the Platform

The wagon rolled steadily toward the Turner family farm, the wheels groaning beneath the weight of bodies, fear, and hope all riding together. Belle sat near Elijah's head, one hand resting gently on his pulse. It fluttered like a frightened bird under her fingertips—weak, uneven, stubborn.

"Lord," she whispered, "steady this heart."

The prayers of the family rose around her—moans that broke open the air, women rocking with grief and faith knitted tightly together.

Elijah's wife, Mrs. Hattie Turner, kept touching her husband's shoulder as though to anchor him to the earth.

"Breathe, Eli," she murmured. "You hear me? You breathe."

Belle watched her for a long moment.

"You love him deeply," she said softly.

Hattie nodded without looking up. "Thirty-four years. Never spent more than three days apart." Her voice wavered. "He ain't allowed to go now."

Belle reached for her hand. "He's fighting. And we're going to help him fight."

Hattie squeezed her fingers. "I know you will. I saw the way you prayed. You pray like someone who knows Him."

Belle managed a tired smile. "I hope so."

Along the Road to the Turner Farm

The road stretched before them—dusty, uneven, bordered by tall grass bending under the breeze. Every now and then, another wagon passed them heading the other direction: settlers, merchants, families seeking homesteads.

Some nodded politely.

Some frowned when they saw Belle among the Turners.

Others stared openly, unsure what to make of a white woman sitting comfortably among Black families in a wagon headed toward farmland rather than church pews.

Belle ignored them.

She kept her focus on Elijah, checking his pulse, his breathing, the color returning—slowly, faintly—to his cheeks.

"He'll need rest," she murmured to Hattie. "No heavy lifting. No stress. And someone must always stay near in case his breath shortens again."

Hattie nodded. "We got plenty hands on the farm. And plenty prayers."

Belle exhaled gratefully. "Good. You'll need both."

A man riding beside the wagon leaned in.

"Doctor?" he said, his voice respectful. "Didn't get your name earlier."

"Annabelle Foster," she replied. "But everyone calls me Belle."

He tipped his hat. "I'm Moses Turner, Elijah's oldest brother. Thank you for stayin' behind."

Belle shook her head. "I didn't do anything extraordinary."

Hattie snorted softly. "Tell that to the folks who jumped off a movin' train to help strangers."

That made Belle laugh, weak but real.

"I did not jump," she protested. "I stepped off firmly."

Moses raised an amused brow. "Miss Belle, that train was blowin' steam. You stepped into a whole new life."

Belle's smile faltered into honesty.

"That seems to be happening a lot lately."

Arrival at the Turner Farm

By mid-afternoon, rolling fields came into view—stretches of open land dotted with chickens, pigs, and rows of early crops. Smoke curled from a woodstove chimney. Several wagons stood nearby, evidence of extended family gathering while some of the men negotiated land purchases in town.

Children ran toward the wagon as it approached.

"Mama! Uncle Eli!"
"What happened?"
"Is he sick? Is he dyin'?"

Belle raised a hand gently. "Give him space. He needs quiet."

The children froze where they were.

Hattie climbed carefully down as the men lifted Elijah from the wagon. Belle followed, wiping sweat from her brow.

"Where to?" Moses asked.

"Hattie's room," Belle said. "With pillows behind his back and a window open. Fresh air—nothing too cold, nothing too hot."

They moved him inside. Belle followed, slipping immediately into the role she never denied—doctor, prayer warrior, determined Samaritan.

Inside, the house smelled of cornbread, woodsmoke, and linen washed with lavender soap. It carried the scent of people who worked hard and made do, but built love into every corner.

They laid Elijah gently on the bed.

Belle sat beside him, unbuttoning the top of his shirt to ease his breathing.

"We'll need broth," she said. "Warm, not hot. Thin enough not to strain the heart."

Hattie nodded. "I'll make it."

She hurried off.

Belle leaned close to Elijah.

"You're not done," she whispered. "Don't you leave her."

His eyelids fluttered in response.

Back in Town — Tension Building

Meanwhile, back at the general store, the conversations continued—loud enough to carry through the thin walls.

"Did you see her? A white woman runnin' around with them folks."
"That ain't proper."
"Doctor? Hah. Women ain't doctors."
"And even if she was—she don't treat coloreds."
"Well, she just did."

"It's shameful," one woman muttered. "Absolutely shameful."

Another disagreed. "Shameful to who? She helped a man. That's more than most did."

"Still," another sniffed, "respectable ladies don't do such things."

Respectable.

Belle hated the word when it was used as a weapon.

Back at the Farm — Prayer and Medicine

Belle worked straight through the afternoon.

She cleaned Elijah's skin with warm cloths, ground herbs she had purchased, mixed a heart-soothing tonic, and instructed the family on how to help him breathe easier.

Moses stood by the door, watching with reverence.

"I didn't know women could do all that," he admitted.

Belle didn't look up. "Women gave you life. Why would it be surprising they can save it too?"

He chuckled under his breath. "You talk bold."

"I act bold," she replied. "Talking is just a bonus."

The family gathered outside the room, praying in waves—voices rising, falling, humming like a supernatural river.

Belle paused once to listen.

She remembered the Native people's quiet, steady prayers that felt like earth breathing.

And she remembered the Romani's frank, questioning prayers that sounded like truth learning to speak.

Now she heard moans, tongues, wails, intercessions—sounds born of history, suffering, hope, and unshakable belief.

Each culture had given her something sacred.

Each had shaped her.

She closed her eyes.

"Lord," she whispered, "heal him. But also… heal the people who think You only listen to one kind of voice."

Evening at the Turner Home

By evening, Elijah's breathing had steadied noticeably.

Hattie returned with broth.

Belle guided her. "Small sips. Let him swallow between each."

They worked together, the rhythm natural, as though they had done it for years.

Not just hours.

When Elijah drifted into deeper, steadier sleep, Belle finally stepped back, exhaustion pulling at every limb.

Moses set a chair behind her. "Sit, Miss Belle. Doctorin' takes strength."

She sank into the chair gratefully.

"How far is the next railroad stop?" she asked.

"A day's ride," Moses said. "But you ain't goin' anywhere tonight."

Hattie shook her head firmly. "You saved my husband. You're stayin' right here."

Belle opened her mouth to protest.

Then stopped.

She was tired.

She was hungry.

And she was needed.

"All right," she whispered. "Just for tonight."

Around the Table

Food was placed before her—cornbread, greens, smoked pork, sweet tea that tasted like summer's best intention.

"You don't have to feed me," she said softly.

"Yes we do," Hattie replied. "It's how we say thank you."

Moses nodded. "We take care of folks who take care of us."

Belle felt warmth spread through her chest.

"Then thank you," she said quietly. "All of you."

The youngest of the children—little Ruthie—leaned forward on her elbows.

"Miss Belle, you a real doctor? For real real?"

Belle smiled. "For real real."

The children giggled.

"Can girls be doctors?" Ruthie asked.

"Yes," Belle said firmly. "Girls can be whatever God tells them to be."

Ruthie's eyes shone. "I wanna be a doctor too!"

Belle ruffled her hair. "Then you will be."

Across the table, the adults exchanged smiles—small, proud, weary from the road but fueled by hope.

Nightfall — A Quiet Conversation

After supper, Moses walked Belle to the small room they arranged for her—a bed with a patchwork quilt, a washbasin, a lantern.

"Miss Belle," Moses said quietly, "town folks ain't too happy 'bout you riding with us today."

Belle raised an eyebrow. "I noticed."

"They'll talk," he warned.

"Let them," she replied. "I didn't come here for their approval."

Moses nodded slowly. "You sure didn't."

He hesitated.

"You got somewhere you're tryin' to get to?"

Belle looked down at her hands.

"Yes," she said. "A calling. A place waiting for me."

"But God keeps detouring you," he said gently.

Belle laughed softly.

"That seems to be His favorite method."

In the Quiet of Night

Later, as the house settled into stillness, Belle sat by the window, lantern low, watching fireflies blink like tiny promises across the fields.

She felt the weight of the day settle deep.

She had left the Native camp.
She had left the Romani caravan.
And now she had stepped off a train into yet another story she had not planned.

"Lord," she whispered into the quiet, "I don't understand the path. But I trust the One leading."

Her eyes drifted shut.

Elijah Turner breathed evenly in the next room.

And Belle, the curvy doctor who kept getting pulled into the lives of people others overlooked, felt peace anchor her again.

She would make it back to her train.

Eventually.

But tonight—

Tonight, she belonged exactly where she was.

CHAPTER TEN

A Place to Heal and Be Healed

Belle stayed with the Turners far longer than she ever intended.

At first, it was Elijah. His heart had been strained close to its breaking point, and though the danger passed, recovery moved with a stubborn slowness that demanded patience, watchfulness, and prayer. Belle monitored him carefully—checking his pulse, listening to his breathing, insisting on rest even when pride urged him otherwise.

"You can't plow a field with a heart still mending," she told him firmly one morning as he tried to stand too quickly.

Elijah grimaced and eased himself back down. "Feels strange sittin' while land waits."

"Land will wait," Belle said. "Your wife will not."

Hattie stood in the doorway, arms crossed, nodding in fierce agreement. "You heard the doctor."

Elijah sighed. "I hear everybody."

Belle smiled. "Good understanding is half the healing."

By the end of the first week, Elijah could walk the length of the porch without breathlessness. By the end of the second, he could sit outside beneath the sun for hours, watching grandchildren chase chickens across the yard and murmuring prayers of gratitude.

But the news traveled faster than Elijah healed.

Word spread quietly at first—passed along fences and fields, carried in wagons and whispered at church doors.

There's a doctor with the Turners.
She stayed behind for one of our own.
She prays before she treats.

Soon, people began coming.

The Community Finds Her

They arrived on foot, in wagons, leading children by the hand or supporting elders by the elbow. Some came cautiously, fear riding just behind hope. Others came boldly, carrying trust like a banner.

A woman arrived with a baby who would not stop crying—fever burning under soft skin. A man came limping, his ankle swollen from years of untreated injury. Another brought a cousin coughing so violently Belle feared broken ribs.

Belle never turned them away.

She worked from morning until dusk, sometimes well into night, her doctor's bag always close, her prayers always spoken plainly.

She saw infections recede. Fevers break. Pain release its grip.

And when healing did not come quickly—when bodies resisted even skill and prayer—she stayed anyway.

"We don't rush God," she told the women gently. "We walk with Him."

Sunday Worship

Sundays were different.

On Sundays, Belle went to church with them.

The church was small—white clapboard, paint faded and peeling, set just far enough down the road to feel separate from town. Several families worshiped there, drawn from surrounding homesteads, filling the space with hums, stomps, claps, and voices that carried suffering and joy in equal measure.

Belle sat among them, head bowed, heart open.

The singing shook the walls.

The prayers shook heaven.

People moaned, wept, lifted hands without apology.

No one minded her accent.
No one measured her body.
No one questioned her past.

They saw her as she was.

After services, the preacher sometimes nodded toward her.

"Doctor Belle," he would say, "you wanna pray for the people?"

Belle never refused.

She laid hands gently, prayed boldly, and stepped back when God moved.

A Blessing on the Land

During her second month with them, the homestead news came.

The men returned from town, papers clutched like treasure.

"They did it," Hattie said breathlessly, pressing the documents into Belle's hands. "They secured the land."

Another homestead joined the Turners'—close enough to share labor, far enough to keep peace. Chickens multiplied. Gardens flourished.

But the greatest blessing was unexpected.

"The railroad's stoppin' here now," Moses announced one evening, eyes shining. "Right in town."

That changed everything.

Chickens could be sold further out. Produce could travel farther than wagons ever could. The land aware and the iron road met, and opportunity bloomed.

They rejoiced—but cautiously.

"Keep every paper," Hattie warned. "Record everything."

Belle learned quickly why.

Someone had already tried to claim a Turner boundary as their own—papers produced mysteriously, accusations leveled coldly.

But the Turners were ready.

They documented. They guarded. They prayed.

"You must protect what God gives you," Belle reminded them. "Wisdom and faith walk together."

A Community That Loved Well

What struck Belle most was the love.

They shared food freely—even when stores were thin.

They shared burdens without counting.

They prayed like they breathed.

They laughed hard.

They welcomed her fully.

She learned dishes she had never tasted—recipes passed through hands and memory rather than books. She learned how spices told stories, how food carried heritage.

She taught them, too.

"Too much lard," she warned one afternoon, smiling as the women groaned playfully. "It'll close those arteries quicker than sin closes a conscience."

They laughed.

"And salted pork?" she continued, wagging a finger. "Raises blood pressure and slows the blood's beat."

"Well, Lord," one woman said dramatically, "there goes all our comfort."

"Oh hush," another replied. "We'll learn new comfort."

Belle showed them how to cook greens lighter, how to render fats carefully, how to season without excess salt.

They teased her mercilessly.

"Oh, look at Doctor Belle," they laughed. "Preachin' health like gospel."

"It is gospel," Belle shot back. "Your body carries the Lord's work. Treat it right."

Working the Land Together

Belle did not hide indoors while others labored.

She hauled water. Gathered eggs. Helped churn butter.

She assisted the men when animals fell ill—diagnosing bloated cows, treating infected hooves, calming a mare with birthing troubles.

"I got medicine for people and creatures," she joked. "God doesn't discriminate by species."

They respected her more for it.

Children followed her everywhere.

"Doctor Belle, look!"
"Doctor Belle, does this hurt?"
"Doctor Belle, pray for my chicken?"

She prayed—sometimes even for the chickens.

"This woman got more faith than fear," Moses said one night.

A People of Faith

Of all the places Belle had been, these people prayed the most fiercely.

They prayed before work. After work. Over food. Over fields. Over fear.

103

They prayed in English, in tongues, in moans and groans too deep for words.

Belle felt strengthened among them.

She no longer felt like the odd one out.

She felt known.

And slowly, inevitably, the question crept in again:

How long will you stay?

She did not know.

But she knew this—

These two months had changed her.

She had been healer and healed. Teacher and student.

And she would carry these people with her, just as she carried the Native community… just as she carried the Romani.

Everywhere God sent her, she left with more love than she arrived with.

She prayed quietly one night beneath the stars.

"Lord," she whispered, "if every stop on this road teaches me this much, I will trust You wherever You lead."

The wind answered softly.

And Belle slept in peace.

CHAPTER ELEVEN

Third Stops Are Never Simple

Belle knew she had stayed as long as she was meant to.

That knowledge did not arrive gently.

It came the way truth often did in her life—quiet, persistent, and impossible to ignore once it settled in her chest.

Two full months had passed since she stepped off that train for Elijah Turner. Two months of healing, praying, cooking, laughing, hauling water, chasing chickens, and learning what community looked like when people loved without reservation.

But her original position still waited.

She had wired again the week before.

Emergency delay. Still coming. Please advise if position remains.

The return telegram came back that morning.

Position waiting. Please come as soon as able.

Belle folded the paper carefully and held it for a long while.

"Well," she murmured, "that settles that."

Letters and Goodbyes

She spent that afternoon writing.

One letter went to her destination—brief, professional, factual. Another went to her parents, carefully worded so as not to alarm them while still telling the truth.

I have been well. I have been needed. I am safe. God has been faithful.

She had written them faithfully every month since leaving home. She knew how worry traveled when left unchecked.

This letter took longer.

She paused often, staring out the window at the Turner land—at the chickens scratching near the fence, at the women laughing near the wash line, at Elijah sitting solidly upright in his chair, arguing cheerfully with Moses about fence posts.

"It's time," she whispered.

She folded the letters and pressed them into Hattie's hands.

"I'll take these to town tomorrow," Hattie promised. Her voice trembled. "You didn't sneak out on us. We appreciate that."

Belle smiled weakly. "I could never."

Church and Collection

That Sunday, the church was full in a way Belle had never seen before.

People came early. They stayed late.

The singing lasted longer.

The prayers grew louder.

When Belle stood to speak, she didn't plan a speech.

Words simply came.

"I didn't come looking for this place," she said honestly. "I came looking for obedience. God gave me both."

There was weeping.

Then the preacher cleared his throat.

"We're takin' a collection," he announced firmly. "For Doctor Belle."

"Oh no," Belle protested immediately. "That's not necessary."

"It is," Hattie said, standing. "And it ain't charity. It's honor."

Money was pressed into her hands—coins, folded bills, small sacrifices made willingly.

"For your ticket," someone said.
"And lunch," another added.
"And just in case," Moses finished gruffly.

Belle cried openly.

Packing Her Off Proper

They packed her food enough to feed a small army.

Healthier food, prepared carefully.

"Don't think we didn't listen," one woman teased. "Less lard, less salt."

Belle laughed through tears. "I'm so proud I could faint."

They presented her with a traveling outfit—sturdy, beautiful, suitable for trains and walking alike.

"And lace underthings," Hattie added briskly. "Because even doctors deserve comfort."

Belle blinked. "Well. I certainly wasn't expecting that."

Hattie smiled sweetly. "Consider it preventative care."

The Station Again

They took her to the railroad station in wagons and carriages.

Children clung.

Adults embraced.

She boarded second class, gripping her doctor's bag like a lifeline.

"I may never see you again," she said softly.

"That don't make this goodbye smaller," Moses replied. "Just deeper."

She waved.

The train pulled away.

Abner Again

"Doctor Belle?"

She turned to see Abner Clay, grinning.

"Well I'll be," he said. "You again."

She laughed. "I promise I'm trying to reach my destination this time."

"I hope so," he replied warmly. "Though the road seems fond of borrowing you."

He tipped his head down the aisle. "I can't linger. Wealthy family aboard—children everywhere."

"Of course," Belle said dryly. "They're always loudest."

The Next Stop

The very next day, they stopped again.

This town was different.

Neater. Quieter. Controlled.

The wealthy family disembarked with authority—fine clothes, servants bustling, children corralled.

Then chaos broke out.

A sharp cry.

A child tripped.

Blood spilled fast and frightening from a head wound.

The father shouted. "Get the doctor!"

"Doctor's away," someone yelled back. "Delivering a baby!"

Abner didn't hesitate.

"Doctor Belle!" he barked.

She was already running.

Doctor Belle Steps In

"I am a doctor," Belle announced firmly as she knelt beside the unconscious boy.

The father hesitated. "I'd prefer a man."

The mother screamed. "My son is bleeding!"

She grabbed Belle's arm. "I'll pay anything. Anything. Just save him!"

Belle was calm. Focused.

"Get me to your house," she instructed. "Two miles is nothing compared to losing time here."

They rushed.

Elegant carriage.
Panicked parents.
Quiet, bleeding child.

The Mansion

The house was breathtaking.

Belle barely noticed.

"Windows open," she ordered. "Light and air."

They placed the boy—Jonathan Hale, aged twelve—on his bed.

Belle stripped cloth quickly, tied pressure bandages, and worked with the nanny, whose stamina impressed her immediately.

"This will require stitches," Belle said calmly. "And I'll have to cut the hair."

The mother nodded desperately. "Do it."

Belle paused only long enough to pray.

"Jesus," she whispered, "guide my hands."

She worked.

Glass fragments removed.
Bleeding controlled.
Stitches placed carefully.

Jonathan breathed steadily.

Hairline would hide the scar.

Belle leaned back finally, exhausted.

"He will live," she said.

Upstairs, relief echoed.

Downstairs, the parents prayed—for the first time that day.

Belle wiped her hands, her mind racing.

She glanced around the elegant room.

Do they know Jesus? she wondered.

Not by words.

But by love.

John 15 echoed in her heart.

Whatever came next, Belle knew one thing—

The road hadn't finished with her yet.

When Belle finally descended the staircase, hands washed and instruments carefully repacked, the parents were waiting at the bottom as though she were royalty rather than a tired doctor with blood faintly staining the cuffs of her sleeves.

The mother rushed forward first.

"He's breathing steadily," Belle said calmly. "The bleeding has stopped. He will wake later with a headache and perhaps a fright—but he will live."

The woman broke down completely.

She pressed her gloved hands to her mouth and sobbed openly, knees buckling just enough that her husband caught her before she could fall.

"Our son," she cried. "Our only child. We nearly lost him."

The father exhaled a breath that sounded as though it had been held for twelve years.

"You saved him," he said thickly. "Whatever you require—whatever sum—name it."

Belle shook her head immediately.

"I don't want your money," she said gently.

The father stared at her, clearly unused to such an answer.

"Doctor, you don't understand," he insisted. "We can compensate you handsomely. This house—this land—"

She raised a hand softly.

"I understand loss," she said quietly. "And gratitude. But money is not what I'm asking for."

The parents exchanged a confused glance.

"Then what?" the mother asked.

Belle took a steady breath.

"If you truly wish to bless me," she said, "then bless others."

They leaned forward, listening.

Belle's Request

"There is a family—the Turners," Belle continued. "Good land, honest people, starting fresh through hard-earned homesteads. I want you to send them two full seasons of assorted seeds. Strong ones. Vegetables, grains. Whatever can take root."

The father frowned slightly, calculating.

"That can be arranged," he said slowly.

"And," Belle added, "I want you to help them transport produce and dried meats on the railroad. Dried fruits as well. They are generous people—they will share. Especially with those who have less."

The mother nodded instinctively.

"There are Native people traveling west," Belle went on, her voice firm now. "On the trail they did not choose. They will need food for winter. They will need it soon."

The father's expression sobered.

"That is… complicated," he said cautiously.

Belle met his eyes evenly.

"You own cattle. Sheep. Wagons. Men. If you can spare livestock to feed a town, you can spare some to keep people alive."

He held her gaze.

Then he nodded once. "Yes. I can arrange that."

Belle felt her throat tighten but pushed on.

"There is also a traveling Romani caravan," she said. "Women, children. They are only a few days' journey from here. They need food. Livestock. Supplies to survive the winter months."

The mother's eyes widened.

"Doctor," she said quietly, "you are asking us to touch many lives we will never see."

Belle smiled faintly.

"That's usually how obedience works."

Silence stretched.

Then the father squared his shoulders.

"It will be done," he said firmly. "Every request. I will notify you when arrangements are complete."

Belle bowed her head briefly—not in relief, but in gratitude.

"Thank you," she said. "That is more than payment enough."

Three Days' Rest

They insisted she stay until the next train.

"It will be three days," the father said. "You've earned rest."

Belle didn't argue.

The mansion, for all its elegance, did not weigh on her as she expected. The staff treated her kindly, respectfully. Meals were brought with care. A quiet room was prepared for her rest.

She spent much of the time checking on Jonathan.

The boy woke the next morning groggy but alive.

"Am I dead?" he mumbled.

Belle smiled. "Very much not."

His grin split across his face. "Father said you're the doctor who fought my head."

She laughed softly. "Your head put up a good fight."

She explained the stitches, the care required, and—when his parents stepped out—whispered a prayer with him.

Unexpected Gifts

On the second day, packages appeared.

Strong boots—well-made, weatherproof.

A heavy coat fit for cold crossings.

A hat with wide brim and sturdy band.

Belle stared at the collection in disbelief.

"I didn't ask for these," she said.

The mother smiled. "You didn't need to."

They brought medicine as well—clean, sealed bottles, supplies she would never have afforded alone.

"For your journey," the father said simply.

Belle swallowed hard.

The Question That Mattered

That evening, as the sun lowered beyond the grounds, Belle joined the parents in the sitting room.

She hesitated—then spoke.

"May I ask you something?" she said gently.

"Of course," the mother replied.

"Do you know Jesus?" Belle asked. "Not by name. But personally."

They exchanged another glance.

"We are Christians," the father said carefully.

Belle nodded. "So many say that. But Jesus said we would know one another by how we love."

She quoted softly, "If ye abide in me, and my words abide in you…"

Their attention sharpened.

"It is not about attendance," Belle continued. "Or reputation. It is about surrender. Trust. Loving others the way He loved."

The mother's eyes filled.

"We have done much," she whispered. "But loved little outside our walls."

Belle reached for her hand.

"You can begin now."

The father bowed his head.

"Tell us what to do."

She did not preach.

She prayed.

They repeated after her—simple words, sincere hearts.

When they finished, the room felt lighter.

The mother smiled through tears. "I feel… free."

Belle smiled gently. "That's Him."

Departure Nears

When the third day came, Abner Clay returned to the station—sure enough on schedule.

"Well, Doctor Belle," he said with a grin, "you finally stayed put long enough to rest."

She laughed. "Just long enough to be delayed again."

He tipped his cap. "Train's ready. This one goes straight."

Belle gathered her things—doctor's bag heavier now, heart heavier still.

The parents embraced her tightly.

"You changed our lives," the mother whispered.

"You saved ours," Belle replied.

The father pressed a folded paper into her hand.

"It's confirmation. Every arrangement."

She squeezed his arm. "Thank you."

As she boarded, Belle looked back once more.

Three days.

Three stops.

Three communities forever stitched into her story.

The train pulled away.

And once again, Belle traveled forward—called, supplied, and ready for whatever waited next.

CHAPTER TWELVE

First Class Doesn't Mean First Called

Belle was on her way once again.

The carriage that carried her back to the railway station moved smoothly over the packed road, pulled by two glossy horses that knew their work and expected obedience in return. The morning air was crisp, and the sky held the pale blue promise of a travel day unmarred by storms—at least not the kind that twisted iron apart.

The wealthy family rode with her this time, seated opposite her in the carriage as though she were an honored guest rather than a woman who had bled into her cuffs for their son only days before.

Jonathan Hale slept soundly at home, stitches healing cleanly along his hairline.

His parents—now locked into Belle's story forever—sat upright and composed, though relief still sat visibly beneath their elegance.

The father was Silas Hale, cattle and sheep magnate, owner of most of the surrounding land and, if town gossip was to be believed, half the town itself.

His wife, Margaret Hale, possessed the sort of composed grace that came from managing both household and reputation with equal discipline.

They had risen early to see Belle safely returned to the rails.

Silas cleared his throat.

"Doctor Foster," he said, "we have taken the liberty of purchasing you a first-class ticket."

Belle blinked.

"A first-class—what?"

"With full dining privileges," Margaret added. "Meals, tea service, proper linens. You will not be cramped or overlooked."

Belle let out a short laugh of disbelief.

"You do realize," she said carefully, "that I've spent the last several months riding in second class, wagons, camps, and once inside a tornado."

Silas smiled faintly. "Precisely why you will ride first class now."

He handed her the envelope.

Belle stared at it.

"Thank you," she said softly. "You didn't need to—"

Margaret took her hand firmly.

"You did not need to save our child either," she replied.

That ended the matter.

Back on the Platform

The station bustled more than the last time Belle had stood there. Crates were stacked for loading, and two conductors argued loudly about schedules. Well-dressed travelers waited impatiently, glancing at watches and each other.

Belle stepped down from the carriage with her doctor's bag over one shoulder and her smaller valise in hand, sturdy boots tapping confidently against the boards.

First class.

She smiled to herself.

"Well," she murmured, "that's new."

The Hales walked her to the gate.

Silas adjusted his coat and cleared his throat again—clearly uncomfortable with goodbyes.

"We have already begun the arrangements you requested," he said quietly. "Seeds. Food shipments. Livestock."

"And the caravan?" Belle asked.

Margaret nodded. "Sent. We hired drivers we trust."

Belle closed her eyes briefly.

"Thank you."

They embraced her then—properly this time, without hesitation.

"You changed us," Margaret whispered.

Belle smiled gently. "You listened."

The whistle blew.

Abner, Again

As Belle stepped onto the train, a familiar voice called out.

"Well I'll be."

She turned to see Abner Clay, resplendent in his porter's uniform, leaning against the rail with a wide grin.

"Doctor Belle," he said, eyes twinkling. "First class now? Why, at this rate you'll be riding the train itself."

She laughed aloud.

"If that happens," she said dryly, "you're welcome to take my luggage."

Abner shook his head in admiration.

"You just don't travel like normal folk," he said. "Storms follow you. Towns stop for you. Now look— private sponsors."

She shrugged. "I just answer when called."

Abner tipped his hat. "That's dangerous work."

The Journey Ahead — Locked In

Belle checked her ticket as she settled into her first-class seat.

Two more days.
Two more stops.

The first stop would be Red Clay Junction, a modest trading town where freight outweighed passengers and the air always smelled faintly of grain and coal.

The second stop would be Willow Bend, a riverside station known for its sawmill and cattle auctions—close enough now that Belle could feel the pull of her destination like a physical thing.

Her final stop awaited beyond that.

Cedar Bluff, Kansas.

A town that had written for her.
A town that waited.

She exhaled slowly.

"So," she murmured, settling back, "after months of detours, I'm almost there."

Dining Car Shock

Belle nearly laughed when she entered the dining car.

White linens. Polished silver. Men in suits murmuring over coffee and newspapers. Women glancing curiously at her sturdy boots and traveling clothes.

She sat anyway.

The waiter blinked when she ordered.

"You're… very certain," he said politely.

"I'm hungry," Belle replied cheerfully.

When the meal arrived—hot, generous, beautifully presented—she bowed her head.

"Thank You, Lord," she whispered. "For reminding me You're not limited by seats or stations."

She ate slowly, savoring both the food and the stillness.

No one needed her at this moment.

That, too, was a mercy.

Reflections in Motion

As the train rocked steadily forward, Belle gazed out the window at passing land—fields giving way to towns, towns slipping back into countryside again.

Native elders walking westward.
Romani women singing beside firelight.
Turner children running barefoot in tall grass.
A bleeding boy saved on a station platform.

So many lives.

So many obediences stacked one atop the other.

She pressed her fingers lightly to her Bible.

"Jesus," she whispered, "I never imagined the road would teach me so much."

What Awaits Her

She would soon meet the ones who had sent for her.

The elder doctor—, a man nearing retirement, brilliant but exhausted.

The mayor—, ambitious, practical, measured in words and influence.

And the sheriff—, watchful, deeply observant, known more for restraint than aggression.

They were expecting a doctor.

They were not expecting Belle.

She smiled faintly at the thought.

"Well," she murmured, "they'll manage."

The train pressed on through the dusk, steam rising like prayer into the cooling sky.

Two more days.

Two more stops.

And then—
Cedar Bluff.

First Class, Five Minutes, and God's Sense of Timing

Belle did not realize how tired she truly was until the train smoothed its rhythm and stopped demanding anything from her.

First class, it turned out, had a way of convincing the body it was finally allowed to rest.

The bedding was soft—truly soft, not the "good enough" softness of boardinghouses or the stiff courtesy of second-class seats. The blankets smelled faintly of soap and steam, and the pillow cradled her neck as if it had been designed for someone who carried weight in both shoulders and spirit.

She slept.

Not the light, alert sleep of a woman accustomed to listening for cries in the night—but the deep, surrendered kind that came only when obedience had caught up to exhaustion.

When Belle woke, morning had already begun its quiet work. Pale light filtered through the curtains. The train rocked steadily forward. Somewhere down the hall, tea cups clinked.

"Well," she murmured, stretching carefully, "this feels downright suspicious."

She dressed slowly, savoring the simple miracle of time not pressing against her chest. In the dining service, a steward smiled kindly and set before her a selection of teas she had never seen together in one place—black, green, herbal blends scented with citrus and spice.

"Take your time, ma'am," he said. "We arrive at our first stop shortly after midday."

Belle almost laughed.

Take your time.

She brought her teacup close, inhaled the warmth, and bowed her head.

"Thank You, Lord," she whispered, "for soft beds, hot tea, and letting me catch my breath."

She read from her Bible after breakfast, lingering in the Gospel of John as the Romani women had promised they would. She underlined one verse lightly, thinking of all the stops and starts, all the people stitched into her story.

Abide in me.

"Yes," she said quietly. "That part I understand."

They were expected to arrive in about thirty minutes now. The stop would be brief—refuel, take on water, let a few passengers off, then onward again toward Red Clay Junction.

Belle felt settled.

Almost suspiciously so.

Which, experience told her, was usually when God cleared His throat.

126

Abner Clay came running.

He did not walk briskly or knock politely. He ran.

"Doctor Belle—Doctor Belle!"

Belle was already on her feet by the time he reached her compartment door.

"What is it?" she asked, calm settling into her bones like armor.

"The sheriff," Abner panted. "Accident. Shot himself in the foot. They're sayin' he's bleedin' bad. Bad enough they're scared."

Belle winced. "How does one accidentally shoot oneself in the foot?"

Abner waved a hand. "Firearm pride mixed with carelessness. Happens more than you'd think."

She reached instinctively for her doctor's bag.

"There's no doctor in the town," Abner continued. "Nearest one's five miles out. They don't think he'll make it before—well."

Belle had already begun pulling on her boots.

"How far are we now?" she asked.

"Five minutes from the station."

She nodded once.

"I'm getting off."

Abner grabbed her smaller luggage and the doctor's bag from her hand as if the motion were choreographed.

"I figured as much," he said. "I'll take these off so the train don't wait. I'll send a telegram to anyone you want at your destination. Tell 'em you're delayed again."

Belle smiled faintly. "They'll stop being surprised eventually."

Abner leaned closer. "There's more."

"There always is," she replied.

He lowered his voice. "Sheriff was supposed to get married today. Mail-order bride arriving on this very train."

Belle froze.

"Oh dear."

"Worse," Abner added. "There are two mail-order brides aboard. Both from the Plus Size Bridal Mail-Order Train."

Belle closed her eyes briefly.

"Of course there are."

The train slowed.

Steam hissed.

The platform came into view.

Abner spoke quickly now. "Sheriff's name is Harlan His intended bride—well—was Lucinda Mae Whitlow. From Ohio."

Locked in.

"And the other?" Belle asked as she stepped toward the door.

"That's Dorothy Belle Vaughn. She was jilted two stops back. Groom never showed."

Locked in.

Abner shook his head. "Lucinda overheard the accident. Says she ain't gettin' off. Told me plain as Sunday she won't nurse a sheriff back from a gunshot wound. Said he might never walk again."

Belle sighed. "And Dorothy?"

Abner let out a breath. "That one's different. She said if the man needs nursing, she'll help you. Says she's a certified nurse. She'll stay till he heals—and then catch her chances down the line."

Belle nodded slowly.

"God's already staffing the room," she murmured.

The train lurched to a stop.

Abner squeezed her arm once. "I hope to see you in a few days, Doctor Belle."

"I'm sure you will," she replied. "The road seems unable to quit me."

She stepped down onto the platform.

The town was small, efficient, and carrying the particular energy of a day that had gone wrong early.

Men clustered. Women whispered. Someone ran past with a bucket of water. Another shouted directions that contradicted the first.

"Where's the doctor?" a voice barked.

Belle pushed forward.

"I'm a doctor," she announced, voice clear, unflinching.

Heads turned.

Someone pointed. "She's the one!"

The sheriff lay on a bench hastily dragged from inside the station office. Blood soaked his boot and pooled darkly beneath his heel.

"Sheriff Harlan," Belle said calmly, dropping to one knee. "Can you hear me?"

He groaned. "If you're here to tell me I've lost my foot, do it quick."

She pressed firm pressure above the wound.

"Then let's make sure you keep it," she replied.

She cut away the boot and sock swiftly.

The wound was ugly, but survivable.

"Who fired the gun?" she asked.

"I did," Harlan muttered. "Cleaning it."

Belle arched an eyebrow. "Firearms should be unloaded before pride gets involved."

A few men snorted despite themselves.

She worked quickly—pressure, elevation, assessment.

"We need clean water," she said. "Boiling, if possible. Cloths. Light."

Someone ran.

Belle felt a presence beside her.

She glanced up.

Dorothy Belle Vaughn stood there, skirts gathered, eyes steady.

"I'm a nurse," Dorothy said quietly. "Trained. Tell me what you need."

Belle nodded. "Good. Stay."

They worked together smoothly, as if they'd practiced for years instead of minutes.

Lucinda Mae Whitlow stood at a distance, arms crossed, hat already adjusted for travel.

"I'm not staying," Lucinda said loudly. "I came to marry a whole man."

Sheriff Harlan groaned. "That's… fair."

Lucinda sniffed. "I wish you well. Truly. But I'm going further west."

She turned and walked back toward the train.

Locked in.

Belle did not judge.

She understood choosing one's limits.

The bleeding slowed.

"Get him indoors," Belle said. "Bed. Windows open."

They carried the sheriff to a nearby residence—the largest in town, chosen more for proximity than elegance.

Inside, Belle finished cleaning the wound thoroughly.

"This will require stitches," she said. "And rest. A great deal of it."

Sheriff Harlan swallowed. "Will I walk?"

"Yes," Belle replied. "Eventually."

He exhaled hard. "Thank God."

She stitched carefully.

Dorothy handed her instruments without being asked. Calm. Capable. Present.

When it was done, Belle stepped back.

"You'll heal," she said. "But you'll listen to your nurses."

Sheriff Harlan glanced between the two women. "I reckon I don't have much choice."

Dorothy smiled faintly. "Not a bit."

Later, when the adrenaline had settled and the sun began its slow descent, Belle stood on the porch, washing her hands in a basin.

The town had quieted.

The train whistle sounded in the distance—moving on without her again.

She smiled to herself.

"Lord," she said softly, "I told You I was settled."

The breeze shifted.

"Next time," she added, "I'll know better."

Behind her, Dorothy joined her at the railing.

"You know," Dorothy said, "I thought I'd be ruined when my groom didn't show."

Belle glanced at her. "And now?"

Dorothy shrugged. "Now I'm nursing a sheriff with an excellent doctor. Feels like a better story."

Belle laughed quietly.

"Most of the good ones do," she said.

The road had paused her again.

But it had not stopped her.

Not even close.

CHAPTER THIRTEEN

A Foot Healed and a Heart Found

Nearly a week had passed since the sheriff's unfortunate meeting with his own firearm, and against all odds—including his own impatience—Sheriff Harlan Harlan was doing remarkably well, now at home.

Belle inspected his foot one morning, fingers firm and confident, brow furrowed with professional seriousness.

"You are healing exactly as expected," she said. "Which is to say—you will live, but you are not invincible."

The sheriff grimaced. "That pain suggests otherwise."

Belle snapped her medical bag shut. "Pain is merely your body expressing an opinion. You do not have to agree with it."

He sighed dramatically.

Dorothy Belle Vaughn, standing just inside the doorway, covered her smile with her hand.

The sheriff noticed.

He always noticed.

Dorothy—Miss Dorothy Belle Vaughn, certified nurse and unexpected gift from a jilted train stop—had become both his salvation and his undoing. She was curvy-curvy in the way that made men forget what they were saying mid-sentence, her flaming red hair braided neatly down her back, freckles scattered boldly across her cheeks like God had been having fun that day.

But it wasn't just her beauty.

She was steady.

Kind.

And entirely unimpressed by his authority.

"Foot up," she said calmly.

"Yes, ma'am," he replied, obeying instantly.

Belle arched a brow. Oh dear, it's already begun.

The Ranch

The Harlan ranch was modest by cattle standards but sturdy and well-run. Several loyal ranch hands came and went throughout the day, each knowing their place and respecting the sheriff not just for his badge but for his fairness.

The house itself was solid, with wide porches and sunlit windows. Once a week, Mrs. Consuela Rivera, the housekeeper, arrived with her apron starched and her opinions sharpened.

She wasted no time.

"You need a wife," she declared one afternoon, pointing at the sheriff as if the matter were already settled. "Men heal faster when married."

"I nearly was," he muttered.

She waved him off. "That one left. This one stayed." She nodded toward Dorothy, who was stirring broth at the stove.

Dorothy nearly dropped the spoon.

Belle bit her lip to keep from laughing.

The Truth He Didn't Expect

The sheriff had filled out the mail-order paperwork because everyone told him he should.

The irony was that once the brides came… he didn't want them.

He wanted the woman changing his bandages.

He called Belle in one afternoon, lowering his voice like a man seeking pardon.

"Doctor," he said carefully, "may I speak freely?"

Belle crossed her arms. "You always do."

He swallowed. "Do you think the nurse might be… inclined toward me?"

Belle studied his face.

The lawman was large, broad-shouldered, handsome in a rugged way that suggested both trouble and safety. But vulnerability had softened him.

"I believe," Belle said slowly, "that God has been arranging more than stitches this week."

Hope flickered in his eyes.

"Would you…" he hesitated. "Would you ask her?"

Belle smiled. "I already intended to."

Dorothy Speaks

Belle found Dorothy later that evening, folding linens with decisive care.

"May I ask you something," Belle said gently.

Dorothy looked up, eyes alert. "That depends."

Belle chuckled. "You've noticed the sheriff."

Dorothy stilled.

"Yes," she said quietly. "I have."

"And?"

Dorothy folded the last towel and set it aside.

"I've fallen in love with him," she said plainly. "But I will not be left again. If he wants me, we go to church today and get married."

Belle blinked. "Today?"

Dorothy nodded. "I will not live in a man's house unmarried, especially not one I already care for. It's not wise—and I do not trust myself."

Belle laughed softly, warmed all the way through.

"That," she said, "is one of the most honest things I've ever heard."

Dorothy lifted her chin. "So—does he want me?"

Belle smiled broadly.

"Yes. Desperately."

The Sheriff Makes His Move

When Belle relayed Dorothy's words, the sheriff didn't hesitate for even a heartbeat.

He reached into his bedside table.

"I already have the ring," he said. "Bought it for the first bride. Guess it was never meant for her."

He called for Jacob Miles, his most trusted ranch hand.

"Ride fast," he ordered. "Get Reverend Thomas Granger. Make sure he brings the license. Quietly."

Jacob grinned. "Yes, sir."

"And Jacob?"

"Yes?"

"Don't tell anyone yet."

Jacob laughed. "Too late, sir. Mrs. Rivera already knows."

When Dorothy came to check his bandages that afternoon, the sheriff took her hand carefully.

"I won't insult you by making speeches," he said. "But I love you. Will you marry me?"

Dorothy laughed and cried at the same time.

"Yes," she said. "Before doubt finds us."

She quoted softly,

"Better is a little with the fear of the Lord than great treasure and trouble therewith." — Proverbs 15:16

"Then let's do this right.

CHAPTER THIRTEEN

A Ring Already Waiting

By the time Reverend Thomas Granger arrived, the ranch already knew.

Not because anyone announced it—quite the opposite—but because joy has a way of traveling faster than secrecy ever could. It slipped through doorways, hopped fences, and rode the wind across the fields until even the horses seemed to sense that something good was about to happen.

Dorothy stood in the small front bedroom, hands clasped tightly together, staring at her reflection in the plain mirror.

"Well," she said softly to herself, "I suppose this is what obedience feels like."

Mrs. Consuela Rivera bustled in behind her, arms full of fabric and authority.

"You are not standing there like a frightened mouse," she declared. "You are about to become a sheriff's wife."

Dorothy swallowed. "In less than an hour."

Mrs. Rivera sniffed. "God does not waste time when He answers prayers."

She adjusted Dorothy's simple dress—nothing extravagant, nothing borrowed from wealth or station. It was clean, pressed, modest, and beautiful in that quiet way that made everything else seem unnecessary.

"You are wise," Mrs. Rivera said as she pinned Dorothy's hair just so. "You did not wait for promises. You asked for covenant."

Dorothy smiled, eyes misting. "I wasn't sure He'd answer so quickly."

Mrs. Rivera laughed. "That is because you think like people do instead of like God does."

In the main room, Sheriff Harlan Harlan sat on the edge of his chair, boot elevated, jaw set in concentration as Belle checked his bandage one final time.

"You are not standing," Belle said firmly.

"I am getting married," he replied. "I can stand."

"You can get married sitting if I say so," Belle shot back. "And you will."

He grumbled but obeyed.

Jacob Miles poked his head in the doorway. "Reverend's here."

The sheriff nodded once, his face utterly sober.

"Send him in."

Reverend Granger removed his hat as he stepped inside, eyes sweeping the room before landing on the sheriff.

"Well," he said mildly, "this is either the quickest courtship I've ever witnessed—or the Lord has been moving ahead of us."

Belle smiled. "Both."

The reverend chuckled. "Where's the bride?"

Mrs. Rivera answered from the hallway. "Walking this way. Behave."

The room stilled as Dorothy entered.

The sheriff's breath caught visibly.

She looked radiant—not because of finery, but because peace had settled on her like it knew her well.

He reached for her hand.

"You sure?" he asked softly.

Dorothy squeezed his fingers. "More than I've ever been."

They gathered in the parlor—no decorations, no music, only the quiet presence of people who knew they were witnessing something holy. Belle stood to one side, hands folded, heart full almost to ache.

She had seen many healings.

This one felt permanent.

The reverend cleared his throat.

"Marriage is not a performance," he said. "It is a covenant before God and witnesses. Today we will not delay joy."

The sheriff swallowed hard.

Dorothy met his eyes steadily.

"Caleb Harlan," the reverend continued, "do you take Dorothy Belle Vaughn—"

Dorothy smiled faintly at her own full name.

"—to be your wife, to love her, cherish her, honor her, and walk with her before God all the days of your life?"

"I do," the sheriff said without hesitation.

"And Dorothy Belle Vaughn," the reverend turned, "do you take Harlan Harlan to be your husband—"

"Yes," she said quickly, then laughed. "I do."

A ripple of gentle laughter passed through the room.

The reverend smiled. "Very well. We'll proceed."

They exchanged vows simply—no flourishes, no promises they could not keep.

Dorothy spoke first.

"I vow to stand with you in weakness and strength. To tell you the truth kindly. To care for you without fear, and to walk faithfully before God with you."

The sheriff's voice was rough when he answered.

"I vow to protect you, listen to you, honor you, and never take for granted the gift of you. I vow to lead our home in humility and faith."

The reverend nodded approvingly.

He took the ring—simple gold, waiting patiently for its true purpose.

"Place the ring," he instructed.

The sheriff slid it onto Dorothy's finger, hands shaking just slightly.

"With this ring," he said, voice low, "I give you my life."

Dorothy whispered, "And I receive it."

The reverend raised his hands.

"What therefore God hath joined together, let not man put asunder." — Matthew 19:6

"I now pronounce you husband and wife."

Dorothy laughed as the words sank in.

The sheriff leaned forward, kissed her gently, reverently.

The room erupted—not in applause, but in praise. Tears, laughter, whispered prayers.

Mrs. Rivera crossed herself and muttered, "Finally."

Later, as the house filled with food and conversation, Belle found herself on the porch again, watching the sun drop low behind the fields.

The sheriff—now husband—joined her, still seated but glowing with a joy no badge could produce.

"You knew," he said quietly.

Belle smiled. "I hoped."

He nodded toward the window where Dorothy stood laughing with the ranch hands.

"I was afraid she'd leave like the others."

Belle shook her head. "She didn't come to be rescued. She came ready."

He absorbed that.

"She won't stay if you don't walk this right," Belle added gently.

He straightened. "Then I'll walk it right."

They sat in companionable silence.

After a moment, he asked, "You leave soon?"

"Yes," Belle replied. "The train will come for me tomorrow."

He frowned. "Figures."

She smiled. "Don't worry. The road knows how to find me."

He chuckled. "That it does."

Dorothy came outside later, slipping her arm through Belle's.

"Thank you," she said softly.

Belle shook her head. "You didn't need me. You were already brave."

Dorothy smiled. "Maybe. But it helped having someone who listens to God like you do."

Belle's eyes misted.

"Well," she said lightly, "you married a man who listens now too. Don't let him forget."

Dorothy laughed. "Never."

As the night settled, Belle returned to her room, heart full, spirit steady.

"Lord," she whispered as she knelt, "You keep surprising me with goodness."

She rose slowly, aware that another chapter was ending.

And another—surely—was about to begin.

The road still waited.

But tonight, joy had caught up with her.

And for once, she wasn't the one boarding the train.

CHAPTER FOURTEEN

Caleb Harlan

Caleb Harlan had married Dorothy Belle Vaughn that day.

And now, for the first time since the vows were spoken, the house was quiet.

The door to his bedroom closed with a soft, unfamiliar sound—final in a way that surprised him. He remained standing for a moment, leaning on his good leg, watching his wife sit carefully on the edge of the bed opposite him.

Dorothy folded her hands in her lap.

Harlan sat slowly across from her, keeping respectful distance between them, his injured foot resting on a stool Belle had insisted upon.

They were married.

And yet they were strangers.

Not uncomfortable strangers—but uncharted ones.

Harlan cleared his throat.

"Well," he said gently, "this is certainly not how I imagined my wedding night."

Dorothy smiled faintly. "Nor I."

The humor eased the air just enough for breath to return.

His Beginning

Harlan had been born big.

His mother used to say God must have been laughing when He stitched him together, because she had never seen a newborn fill a cradle the way he had. He grew faster than other boys, broader, heavier, stronger—sometimes to his father's quiet concern, often to the envy of others.

But bigness never frightened him.

Cruelty did.

Harlan grew up on land that demanded honesty. His father had been a lawman of sorts—unofficial, unpaid, respected because he was fair and feared because he was not easily swayed. When disputes rose, men came to the Harlan property before they went anywhere else.

"Justice starts at home," his father used to say.

Harlan learned early that strength was meant to protect, not intimidate. He learned to sit quietly before speaking and to finish what he started even when no one was watching.

When his father died suddenly—too young, too fast— the town did something unexpected.

They asked Harlan to step in.

He was barely thirty.

"I'm not ready," Harlan had said.

"We're not asking for ready," the mayor replied. "We're asking for right."

Harlan took the badge because the town needed him.

And because saying no felt like abandoning something God had already placed in his hands.

The Sheriff's Loneliness

Being sheriff was a strange loneliness.

Everyone knew his name.

Few knew his heart.

He spent his days mediating disputes, keeping peace, disciplining when necessary, and walking carefully along a line that could shift beneath his feet at any moment.

Men respected him.

Women watched him.

Children trusted him.

But when he returned to the ranch at night, the house was silent except for the creak of wood and the sound of wind passing through tall grass.

He told himself solitude was peace.

But peace and isolation are cousins, not twins.

Harlan wanted a home.

Not just a house.

He wanted laughter that did not echo unanswered. A table where dishes did not remain untouched. A woman who would speak truth to him without fear and pray for him when his strength ran thin.

That was why he filled out the mail-order forms.

Not because he lacked courage—but because he lacked opportunity.

He had underestimated God.

The Injury That Changed Him

When he shot himself in the foot, the pain was immediate—but the humility was worse.

He had been careless.

And carelessness nearly cost him everything.

Lying there, bleeding on the station platform, he remembered thinking—not I'm dying—but I never finished the life I was called to live.

Then Dr. Belle appeared.

And after her came Dorothy.

Harlan had noticed her from the beginning.

Not because she was beautiful—though she was—but because she was calm when others faltered. Because she did not flinch at blood or authority. Because she corrected him gently and expected obedience not because he was sheriff, but because she was right.

He had never been tended with patience before.

Never been spoken to firmly without shame.

Never felt seen in stillness.

Somewhere between the stitching and the long nights, affection rooted itself.

He did not fight it.

He prayed over it.

Sitting Across From His Wife

Now, seated across from Dorothy Belle Vaughn, Harlan studied her with reverence.

"I should tell you who you married," he said quietly.

Dorothy nodded. "I'd like that."

So he told her.

He told her about his parents. About the badge. About the fear of getting things wrong and the greater fear of standing still. About the nights when he felt his life waiting for a sound that never came.

"I didn't marry you out of loneliness," he said firmly. "I married you because I believed God entrusted you to me."

Dorothy's eyes shone.

"I didn't come to be rescued," she replied softly. "I came ready to stand."

Harlan exhaled, something loosening deep in his chest.

"I may stumble," he said. "I may be stubborn. But I will never make you invisible."

That mattered to her.

She nodded once. "Then we'll do well."

They sat there—two people married by obedience, now learning intimacy through truth.

Outside, the ranch settled into night.

And for the first time in years, Harlan Harlan felt like the silence had an answer.

Dorothy Belle Vaughn

Dorothy Belle Vaughn had been married less than an hour, and already her life felt nothing like she had imagined.

She sat on the bed opposite her new husband, skirts smoothed carefully beneath her hands, spine straight, heart full and trembling all at once. The room felt different now—not because furniture had moved or vows had been spoken, but because purpose had entered and refused to leave.

She was no girl.

She was a woman who had lived long enough to know disappointment, and brave enough to believe again anyway.

Harlan Harlan watched her quietly, giving her the gift of space. That mattered to her more than he knew.

After a moment, she spoke.

"I suppose it's my turn," she said, voice warm, steady. "To tell you who I am."

Harlan nodded. "I'd like that very much."

Dorothy had been born into a household that valued usefulness over tenderness.

Her mother loved her, but efficiency came first. Her father believed affection should be earned through reliability, not given freely. Dorothy learned early how to carry responsibility without complaint—and how to tuck away her longing where it would not trouble anyone.

She had always been curvy.

151

Not the delicate kind of pretty that slipped through rooms unnoticed—but the kind that filled space unapologetically. Some people loved her for it. Others seemed determined to correct her for it.

She learned not to shrink.

She became a nurse because healing felt like calling, not career. People trusted her. Sick rooms did not frighten her. Pain made sense in a way rejection never had.

And yet—despite her competence, her faith, her kindness—romance had not been kind to her.

She had been promised once.

Not publicly, not formally, but in words that sounded sincere at the time. She had believed them. She had rearranged her hopes quietly to make room.

Then he vanished.

When she boarded the Plus Size Bridal Mail-Order Train, it was not desperation that placed her there—it was decision.

"I will move forward," she had told God. "Or I will stay where I am and turn bitter. I choose forward."

She did not expect forward to look like a wounded sheriff and a hurried wedding.

But here she was.

Dorothy looked at Harlan now—large, broad-shouldered, resting carefully to protect his healing foot. The strength in him was obvious. The gentleness surprised her more.

"I've never wanted to be chosen by accident," she said quietly. "Or convenience. Or fear."

Harlan met her gaze fully.

"You were not," he said. "You were chosen by obedience."

Her breath caught.

"That," she replied softly, "means more to me than romance."

Silence settled comfortably again, not awkward but attentive.

Dorothy stood then, moved to the small table near the window, and picked up a Bible Belle had left behind—a quiet gift without commentary.

She returned and held it between them.

"Would you read with me?" she asked.

Harlan nodded. "Always."

She opened to a marked place and smiled faintly.

"Song of Solomon," she said. "Chapter four."

Harlan chuckled gently. "That's bold reading for the first evening."

Dorothy smiled back. "I don't mean it immodestly. I mean it honestly."

She read aloud, voice low and reverent:

'Behold, thou art fair, my love; behold, thou art fair.'

Harlan listened—not as a man startled by intimacy, but as one learning how Scripture could be lived, not just quoted.

She continued:

'Thou hast ravished my heart, my sister, my spouse; thou hast ravished my heart with one of thine eyes…'

She closed the Bible then and rested it on her lap.

"This book," she said, "is not about shame. It's about covenant. Seeing fully. Choosing completely."

Harlan swallowed.

"I don't know much about poetry," he admitted. "But I know when something rings true."

She smiled. "Then we'll read it slowly. Together."

Later, as lamplight softened the corners of the room, Dorothy surprised herself by speaking again—not nervously, but with hope.

"Do you want children?" she asked.

Harlan blinked.

Then smiled—wide, honest, unguarded.

"I've imagined them," he said. "Running through the fields. Loud. Curious. Asking too many questions."

Dorothy laughed softly. "I imagine teaching them. Bandaging scraped knees. Praying over their beds."

He shifted carefully toward her, still mindful of his injury, and reached for her hand.

154

"We'll raise them knowing who they are," he said. "And Whose they are."

Dorothy nodded, tears shimmering but not falling.

"I've waited a long time to be spoken to like that," she admitted.

Harlan squeezed her fingers. "I've waited a long time to mean it."

They sat there, hands joined, not rushing what God was clearly building with intention.

There was no fear in the room.

Only wonder.

Dorothy leaned her head slightly toward his shoulder— not fully resting, but close enough to signal trust.

"Thank you for marrying me today," she said quietly. "Even though we don't yet know all the ways our lives fit."

Harlan smiled.

"We'll discover them."

Outside, the ranch breathed gently under the stars.

Inside, a marriage settled—rooted not in urgency, not in fantasy, but in covenant.

And for Dorothy Belle Vaughn, who had once boarded a train uncertain if anyone would ever choose her—

She had not only been chosen.

She had been known.

And tomorrow, life would begin in earnest.

155

CHAPTER FIFTEEN

The goodbyes came quicker than Dorothy expected.

There were embraces—long and lingering ones—as if no one wished to be the first to let go. Dr. Belle stood steady at the station, her doctor's bag secure at her side, eyes bright with that familiar mixture of peace and readiness that always appeared when God moved her forward again.

Dorothy held her close.

"You changed my life," Dorothy said quietly.

Belle smiled, the kind of smile that carried both humility and certainty. "God did that. I just kept showing up."

Harlan stood a few steps away, hat in hand, his injured foot resting carefully against the platform edge. He extended his hand to Belle, then thought better of it and pulled her into a brief, strong embrace.

"You saved my foot," he said. "And you brought me my wife."

Belle laughed softly. "I'll consider that advanced fieldwork."

The train whistle sounded, sharp and final.

Dorothy watched as Belle boarded, waving until the last car disappeared from sight. The ache that followed was gentle but real—the familiar feeling of watching someone God had sent move on exactly when they were meant to.

"Well," Harlan said quietly beside her, "it's our turn now."

Dorothy nodded, heart steady. "Yes. It is."

Later that morning, after the house quieted and the last visitors departed, Harlan motioned toward one of his ranch hands waiting by the gate.

"Elias," he called. "If you're free, take my wife around. Show her the land."

"Yes sir," the man replied warmly.

His name was Elias Carter, and it settled easily into memory as trusted names always did.

Elias Carter was a Black man near Harlan's age—tall, broad-shouldered, with a calm authority shaped by prayer and years of honest labor. His eyes carried both kindness and discernment, the look of a man who knew his purpose and walked in it daily.

Dorothy noticed how naturally Harlan spoke to him, how much respect passed between them without display.

"Mrs. Harlan," Elias said with a gentle smile, "ready to meet the ground that keeps us fed?"

Dorothy returned the smile. "Very much so."

Before they rode out, Elias guided the wagon toward town.

"You'll want supplies first," he explained. "A household don't breathe right till it's stocked."

Dorothy laughed lightly. "I was thinking the same thing."

The general store smelled of wood, coffee, and flour dust. Elias was greeted like family. The storekeeper nodded approvingly when he saw Dorothy.

"So this is her," he said. "Welcome, ma'am."

Dorothy thanked him and began selecting what she would need—flour, sugar, jars, spices, linens, baking tools. She paused before a stack of pie tins and smiled to herself.

"These will do nicely."

Elias chuckled. "Sheriff's about to discover he married well."

Dorothy placed everything on her husband's tab just as Harlan had instructed. She felt no guilt—only gratitude. She was starting fresh, and she intended to build wisely.

As they drove back toward the ranch, Elias explained how things had worked before.

"My wife, Clara, cooked for Harlan three days a week," he said. "Good woman, but it took a toll. Three children already, and another on the way."

He laughed, pride filling his voice. "Yes ma'am. We stay fruitful."

Dorothy smiled warmly. "That is a blessing."

"It is," Elias agreed. "And now Clara won't have to carry that load anymore."

"I love to cook," Dorothy said. "Especially baking."

Elias nodded knowingly. "That part of your reputation arrived before you did."

She laughed outright. "Then I hope my husband enjoys dessert."

"I don't think he's prepared," Elias replied with amusement.

They rode through open pasture, cattle grazing lazily, fences mended and strong. Elias gestured toward a stretch of land nearby.

"Harlan deeded me five acres," he explained. "Sold me the house my family lives in—fair and honest."

Gratitude softened his voice.

"He's a good man," Elias continued. "He loves all races. Sometimes folks make that harder than it should be—but he never turns away from what's right."

Dorothy listened carefully.

"I'm grateful for him," she said.

Elias smiled. "And he's grateful for you."

They passed the small cottage where Elias lived with his wife and children. A little girl waved from the porch, curls bouncing. Dorothy waved back, heart warming instantly.

"I hope we start a family soon," Dorothy said softly, more prayer than plan. "I'm already thirty."

Elias nodded thoughtfully. "Timing belongs to God. Joy belongs to us."

When they returned to the ranch house, Dorothy stepped down from the wagon and looked across the land again.

Home.

"I must write my parents," she said suddenly. "They should hear this from me."

Elias nodded. "They'll hear happiness between every line."

Dorothy smiled, excitement settling into something deeper—something lasting.

A husband.
A home.
Land beneath her feet.

And the quiet certainty that God was not finished—He was establishing.

Caleb Harlan had enforced the law in that county for nearly a decade.

He had stared down armed men, broken up brawls, mediated disputes that could have ended in bloodshed, and signed papers that changed the course of other people's lives. He had buried friends, sworn in deputies, and stood alone more times than he cared to remember.

None of that unsettled him the way walking back into his house now did.

Not because it frightened him—but because it mattered.

Dorothy moved through the rooms with a quiet curiosity, fingers brushing tabletops, eyes lingering on corners of the house as if listening for what had once lived there. Harlan watched her from the doorway, leaning his weight carefully, mindful of his healing foot.

160

She fit.

Not as decoration.

As purpose.

"You don't have to stand there like that," she said gently, sensing him without looking back. "This is our house now."

Our.

The word lodged in his chest with unexpected force.

"I know," he replied. "Just realizing it."

She smiled and continued unpacking small things—linens, a few books, kitchen tools that already felt like promises rather than objects.

Harlan cleared his throat.

"I should probably tell you a few things," he said. "Before someone else does."

Dorothy turned and leaned lightly against the table, attentive.

"All right."

He told her about the ranch hands—who drank too much, who prayed quietly, who worked hard and never complained. He told her which fences needed tending every spring, which cattle were prone to wandering, which neighbors needed patience more than authority.

He told her about the town.

Who would welcome her.

Who would test her.

161

"And who," he added carefully, "will never think kindly of me choosing what's right over what's easy."

Dorothy didn't flinch.

"I didn't marry ease," she said. "I married calling."

Harlan studied her for a long moment.

"I'm not a gentle man by nature," he said honestly. "I've learned restraint, but it came through effort."

She nodded. "I don't require softness. I require integrity."

That was a relief he hadn't known how to ask for.

Later, they walked the land together—slowly, deliberately.

Harlan explained where he planned to expand fencing, where he hoped to add another barn. He told her how he dreamed of creating a place where men could work honestly and families could live without fear.

"I don't want this ranch to thrive at the expense of anyone," he said. "That's never been my way."

Dorothy slipped her arm through his carefully.

"And I don't want my home to run on pride," she replied. "That's never been mine."

They paused near the edge of the pasture where the land dipped gently.

"I want children," Harlan admitted quietly, as if confessing something sacred. "Laughter. Noise. Life."

Dorothy smiled. "I want a table that's always full."

He chuckled. "That explains the baking reputation."

"It's ministry," she replied solemnly.

They both laughed.

That evening, as the sun lowered, Dorothy prepared supper—simple, hearty, done with confidence. Harlan sat nearby, pretending to read but mostly watching her move through the kitchen as if she had always belonged there.

When they prayed together before eating, it was unpolished and sincere.

"Thank You for bringing us together," Harlan said simply. "Teach me to love her well."

Dorothy added softly, "Teach me to build with him, Lord."

They ate in comfortable silence.

Afterward, as lamplight softened the room, Harlan fetched his Bible and sat beside her.

"Belle used to say," he began, "that Scripture reads differently when you're ready to live it."

Dorothy nodded. "She's right."

They opened together to Song of Solomon.

Harlan read first—slow, steady, unembarrassed.

"Many waters cannot quench love, neither can the floods drown it…"

Dorothy finished the verse, smiling.

"If a man would give all the substance of his house for love, it would utterly be contemned."

They closed the book.

"This," Harlan said quietly, "is not possession. It's protection."

Dorothy leaned her head gently against his shoulder, careful of his injury but unafraid of closeness.

"We'll grow into this," she said.

"I intend to," he replied.

Outside, the ranch settled into night.

Inside, Harlan Harlan—sheriff, rancher, husband—felt the unfamiliar peace of knowing he was no longer walking alone.

And for the first time, the future didn't feel heavy.

It felt shared.

When you are ready, we can move forward into Chapter Sixteen:

Belle arriving at her long-awaited position

Or Dorothy adjusting to town life as a sheriff's wife

Or the two storylines weaving together again

Just tell me where to go next.

CHAPTER SIXTEEN

Dorothy Harlan had not gone looking for another calling.

It found her anyway.

The very morning after the wedding—while the echoes of joy still lingered in the corners of the house—Mrs. Dorothy Harlan stepped into a role she had carried before but never quite like this. She was no longer simply a nurse passing through or a woman helping in crisis. She was now the woman people were turning toward when there was nowhere else to go.

There was no doctor in town.

And word had spread fast.

It began innocently enough.

One wagon arrived early, just after sunrise, carrying a basket of eggs still warm from the henhouse.

"Just checkin' on the sheriff," the farmer said politely.

Then another appeared with a pie—apple, neatly latticed, steam still rising.

Then another with a chocolate cake carefully wrapped in cloth.

By the time the sun had climbed a hand's breadth above the horizon, the road to the Harlan ranch looked like market day.

Sheriff Harlan stood at the window in his stocking feet, one hand braced on the frame, staring out in disbelief.

"Why," he asked slowly, "does it look like the entire county has decided to visit today?"

Mrs. Consuela Rivera, the housekeeper, peered past him and clucked knowingly.

"They are not here for you," she said. "They are here for her."

Harlan frowned. "For Dorothy?"

Mrs. Rivera nodded. "They heard. Nurse. No doctor. People talk."

Harlan felt something twist in his chest—not jealousy exactly, but something sharper, more complicated.

He turned his head just in time to see Dorothy crossing the yard, skirts gathered, sleeves rolled, her movements purposeful and calm. She wasn't headed toward the house.

She was headed toward the barn.

"What is she doing?" he demanded.

Mrs. Rivera did not look at him. "Being who she is."

By midmorning, Dorothy had already seen more people than she had expected in a week.

The barn had been cleaned the night before in anticipation—fresh straw laid down, water boiled and cooled, benches dragged into place. She worked with quick assurance, listening closely, asking careful questions, examining swollen joints, flushed skin, worried bellies.

She treated fevers.

She soothed nerves.

She whispered prayers without ceremony.

One woman clutched her arm, eyes wide. "I woke up bleeding. Am I losin' my baby?"

Dorothy stayed steady. "No. Sit. Breathe. We'll take this one step at a time."

Another man limped in, embarrassed. "Sheriff said you wouldn't turn me away."

Dorothy met his eyes kindly. "He's right."

Soon, the truth came into full view.

The pies and cakes were not visits.

They were offerings.

Under them came complaints—pain that had lasted too long, fevers ignored because there was no doctor to call, early labor pains, infected cuts, aching lungs, trembling hands.

There were even Native women—quiet, watchful—standing near the edge of the barn, waiting patiently until Dorothy beckoned them forward.

The line of wagons lengthened.

The work did not slow.

Inside the house, Sheriff Harlan paced.

Carefully—but furiously.

He could see the wagons from the front porch now, could hear voices and murmurs drifting on the breeze. He could see Dorothy moving steadily among them, her face composed, her hands confident.

"She just got married," he muttered. "She just became my wife."

Mrs. Rivera folded laundry unbothered. "And yesterday she was a nurse before God."

Harlan rubbed his face.

"I need my wife," he said. "My foot is still healing. I haven't even taken her walking yet."

Mrs. Rivera looked up then. "Did you marry a woman to keep her hidden?"

He froze.

"No," he said quietly.

"Then you married the whole woman," she replied.

That struck harder than anger.

He lowered himself into a chair and bowed his head.

"I need to pray," he said.

He prayed—but the answer did not come quickly.

Not the way he wanted.

He prayed for protection.

He prayed for patience.

He prayed for wisdom that felt just out of reach.

He wanted to walk out there and pull Dorothy back into the house, close the doors, make the world wait.

But he knew her heart.

She would not turn anyone away.

And that knowledge made it worse.

He sat in silence until an older woman came hurrying to the porch.

"Sheriff," she called anxiously, "your wife is extraordinary."

"I know," Harlan said flatly.

"But there's more," she added. "One woman's in labor. Early. She's scared."

His jaw tightened.

"Did you ask her to wait?" he demanded.

The woman blinked. "No sir. Mrs. Harlan is already with her."

Harlan leaned back and stared at the ceiling.

"Why did the doctor have to leave?" he whispered.

Belle.

Dr. Belle.

The name stirred something in him.

He remembered now—clearly.

Henry College.

That was where she had trained.

That was where she had received her medical education.

He stood abruptly.

"If there's no doctor here," he said aloud, "then I will find one."

Mrs. Rivera glanced up. "You mean to write for one?"

"I do," he answered firmly. "Today."

Harlan made his way slowly to his desk.

Each step was steadier now. The foot was healing—slowly, faithfully.

Just like marriages did.

He sat and pulled a fresh sheet of paper toward him.

"Lord," he prayed quietly, "I need help. And I need it without breaking what You've built."

He dipped his pen and began to write.

To Henry.

To the school that had shaped the woman who had brought life into his own house and then carried it forward into the town.

He paused, listening to the distant sounds of the barn—voices, murmurs, the low cry of a woman in labor answered by Dorothy's calm reassurance.

He closed his eyes.

"I'll talk to her," he said softly. "But not yet."

For now, he would wait.

He would pray.

And he would send that letter.

Because loving a woman like Dorothy Harlan meant learning when to hold close—

And when to build room around her calling.

Dorothy Harlan did not look up when the sheriff finally entered the barn.

She did not need to.

She knew the rhythm of his steps now—the careful favoring of the healing foot, the slight pause before each shift of weight. Even among the murmurs of voices and the low cries of discomfort, she recognized him as easily as breathing.

"Sheriff," someone said urgently, stepping aside. "She's inside with the young woman."

Harlan nodded and kept walking.

The barn had become something else entirely. What had been a place for hay and tack now held benches, clean cloths, kettles warming over small fires, and a quiet order that moved without his permission yet without chaos. It unsettled him—and humbled him—in equal measure.

Dorothy knelt beside a young woman half-reclined on straw and blankets. Her face was damp with sweat, her hands clenched tightly in the folds of her dress.

"You're doing well," Dorothy said calmly. "These are early pains, not birth yet. Breathe through them."

The woman nodded, tears sliding down her face. "I was scared. There ain't no doctor."

"I'm here," Dorothy replied gently. "And you are not alone."

Only then did Dorothy glance up.

She saw Harlan standing just inside the doorway, tall even when resting his weight, hat in hand, his face a mix of worry, frustration, and something much deeper.

She held his gaze for a heartbeat—long enough to acknowledge him, not long enough to invite interruption.

Then she turned back to her patient.

Harlan stepped back outside.

It was the hardest thing he had done in weeks.

He leaned against the barn wall, folded his arms, and closed his eyes.

Lord, he prayed, I didn't know loving someone could feel like standing still while the world leans on them.

He stayed there longer than he planned.

Eventually, Mrs. Rivera joined him, wiping her hands on her apron.

"She is strong," the housekeeper said. "But even strong women need structure."

Harlan nodded slowly. "That's what I'm praying for."

By late afternoon, the line had thinned.

People began to drift away—relieved, reassured, instructed. Some left lighter. Some left still worried but hopeful. Almost all left something behind.

Baskets. Jars. A sack of flour. A small carved token pressed awkwardly into Dorothy's palm by a Native woman who spoke little but meant much.

When Dorothy finally stepped into the open air, her shoulders sagged.

Harlan was beside her instantly.

"You're exhausted," he said.

She smiled faintly. "Yes."

"You didn't eat."

"No."

"You didn't rest."

"No."

He took a breath. "Dorothy."

She looked up at him fully now.

"I know," she said quietly.

They stood there, married less than two days, already facing a problem neither had named but both understood.

He gestured toward the house. "Let's talk."

Inside, they sat at the small table where they had prayed together the night before.

Harlan did not raise his voice.

He did not demand.

Instead, he spoke carefully—as one learning a language that mattered.

"I was angry today," he admitted. "Not at you. At the situation."

Dorothy nodded. "I felt it."

"I missed you," he continued. "I wanted this day to belong to us. I wanted to walk you around the land, talk about small things, laugh without interruption."

Her eyes softened. "I wanted that too."

"But," he said, steadying himself, "I married a woman who does not turn people away."

She swallowed. "I didn't plan for this."

"I know."

He reached across the table, taking her hands.

"So I wrote a letter," he said. "To Henry. To see if they would send a doctor. Or recommend one willing to come."

Dorothy blinked. "You did?"

"I did," he said. "Because this cannot all rest on your shoulders."

Tears filled her eyes—not from exhaustion, but from relief.

"Thank you," she whispered.

He squeezed her hands gently. "We will build boundaries. Together. Not walls. Doors."

She smiled through tears. "That sounds like you."

They sat quietly.

Then Dorothy spoke again.

"I will not stop helping," she said softly. "But I will not do this alone."

Harlan nodded. "Good. Because I need my wife too."

She laughed quietly. "Then we must schedule each other."

"Imagine that," he replied dryly. "Courtship with appointment times."

That made her laugh fully.

That evening, they walked slowly along the edge of the land, the sunset spilling gold across the pasture.

Harlan told her what little he remembered of Belle—her schooling, her confidence, the authority she carried without asking permission.

"She trusted God with movement," Dorothy said thoughtfully. "I trust Him with staying."

Harlan smiled at that.

When they returned to the house, Dorothy prepared a simple meal. They ate together without interruption. When they prayed, it felt steadier—less urgent, more rooted.

Later, as lamplight softened the room again, Dorothy leaned against him, careful of his foot.

"You did the right thing today," she said. "Even when you didn't have the answer."

He rested his head lightly against hers. "So did you."

Outside, the ranch settled into night.

The barn stood quiet.

And inside the Harlan house, something stronger than frustration took shape—not resolution, not certainty, but partnership.

Tomorrow would come with its own demands.

But tonight, they were learning how to stand together in the middle of calling.

And that, they both sensed, was how everything else would be healed.

The next morning, Dorothy did not step back into the barn until after she prayed.

She stood just outside the wide doors, the smell of hay and earth thick in the warm afternoon air, hands braced on the rough wood as she bowed her head.

"Lord," she whispered, voice low so only Heaven would hear, "I cannot be everything to everyone. But I can be obedient. Order my steps. Give me wisdom that does not exhaust the well You are building in me. Teach me when to stay, and when to step back."

She opened her Bible—the small one she kept tucked in her medical bag—and read quietly, anchoring herself before returning to the work.

"Come unto me, all ye that labour and are heavy laden, and I will give you rest."
—Matthew 11:28

She closed her eyes.

"Yes," she murmured. "That includes nurses, too."

When Dorothy walked back inside, the air had shifted. People noticed. They always did when someone returned not frantic, but centered.

The woman in early labor had settled, breathing more evenly now. An elderly man sat with his boot off, ankle propped up, grumbling less. A young boy with a fever slept against his mother's shoulder.

Word had begun to spread through the town—not just that Mrs. Harlan was a nurse, but that she prayed before she touched you, that she listened more than she spoke, that she did not rush pain away as if it were an inconvenience.

People noticed that too.

A man lingered near the barn door, hat clutched nervously in his hands.

"Ma'am," he said hesitantly, "I don't rightly need a doctor… just thought I might."

Dorothy smiled softly. "Sit down anyway."

Outside, the town reacted in waves.

Some were grateful.

Some were suspicious.

Some were quietly ashamed.

"She's doin' what the church ought to be doin'," one woman whispered as she passed by the fence.

Another shook her head. "A sheriff's wife ought to stay inside."

Others, emboldened by her steadiness, spoke more freely.

"There ain't been help like this since old Doc Fletcher died."

"If she leaves, we're sunk."

By the time dusk approached, the barn felt heavy—not with sickness, but with expectation.

Dorothy felt it in her bones.

This could not continue without change.

Inside the house, Harlan knelt.

Not beside the bed.
Not in a chair.
On the floor.

The sheriff removed his hat and pressed his forearms into it, breathing slowly as he prayed—not loudly, not with flourish, but with the honesty of a man who had reached the edge of his own ability.

"Lord," he said quietly, "I married a woman You called before You gave her to me. I need wisdom that does not cage her, and structure that does not crush us. If I act in fear, correct me. If I act in pride, stop me."

He opened his Bible to Psalms without choosing the page.

"Except the Lord build the house, they labour in vain that build it."
—Psalm 127:1

Harlan exhaled heavily.

"So build it," he said. "Because I don't know how alone."

By the time Dorothy returned to the house, dust on her hem and tired resolve in her eyes, Harlan was ready—not with demands, but with resolve.

They sat together at the table again.

"This town," Dorothy said quietly, "is hurting."

Harlan nodded. "I see that."

"They haven't had consistent medical care. They don't know where to turn."

"And you did not become a solution," Harlan replied carefully. "You became a lifeline."

She met his eyes. "That's the danger."

They sat in silence for a moment, the weight of shared understanding growing heavier instead of lighter.

"I spoke to some of the women," Dorothy continued. "They expect me to be available every day. All hours."

Harlan tightened his jaw—not in anger, but concern.

"You cannot," he said firmly. "And you will not."

She studied his face.

"Tell me why," she said—not defensively, but honestly.

"Because God did not call you to replace a doctor," Harlan replied. "He called you to serve until order was restored."

That stopped her.

He leaned forward slightly.

"And because I did not marry you to lose you to exhaustion."

Tears rose suddenly, uninvited.

She wiped them away with the back of her hand.

"I don't want to abandon them."

"You won't," Harlan said. "But you also won't bleed out for them while I stand by and call it faith."

She let out a shaky breath.

"So what do we do?"

He reached for her hands.

"We bring order. Set days. Set hours. Train helpers. And we pray that Henry answers."

That night, word reached the ranch that a young mother had delivered safely.

"Thank You, Jesus," she whispered. "For life. For mercy. For limits."

Back at the ranch, a few townspeople lingered near the fence even after dark, whispering among themselves.

"She didn't turn anyone away—but she didn't let chaos rule either."

"That's different."

"That's God-ordered."

By candlelight, Dorothy and Harlan read together before sleep.

She chose the passage this time.

"Two are better than one; because they have a good
reward for their labour."
—Ecclesiastes 4:9

She leaned her head against his shoulder.

"We will figure this out," she said.

"Yes," he replied. "We will."

Outside, the town quieted for the night.

Inside, a marriage strengthened—not by ease, but by
obedience shaped with prayer.

And in Heaven's ledger, something had been written
that day:

Not she carried the town—
But they carried the calling together.

CHAPTER SEVENTEEN

Belle was finally back on the train.

Not delayed.
Not diverted.
Not stepping off because the road demanded her again.

She was moving forward.

First class suited her in a way that surprised her—not because of luxury itself, but because rest had become an act of obedience rather than indulgence. The seat was wide and cushioned, the bedding freshly pressed and changed daily, the windows large enough to let the land unfold like a living map. Attendants passed quietly, offering warm meals served on proper china, real silverware, and linen napkins that folded neatly instead of slipping onto the floor.

Belle smiled to herself.

"Well," she murmured, settling in, "this feels almost suspiciously peaceful."

She enjoyed hot baths brought in copper basins, fresh towels scented lightly with soap and lavender, and regular access to the dining car where the food arrived hot and plentiful. Breakfasts of eggs and fresh bread. Soups simmered slowly. Meats carved carefully. Fruit served without bruises.

And the teas.

Belle lingered over them most of all.

Strong black tea in the mornings.
Green tea with light honey after meals.
Chamomile in the evenings to quiet her thoughts.
Peppermint for digestion.

A fragrant amber-colored rooibos that reminded her strangely of open fields at sunset.

She gave thanks for every cup.

She had two days left.

Just two.

For the first time since boarding months ago, the destination no longer felt theoretical. It was close enough now that she could imagine the station platform, the faces waiting, the conversations she would soon have with the older doctor and the town officials who had written for her.

She opened her Bible each morning and read quietly, savoring the stillness.

"The steps of a good woman are ordered by the Lord."

"Yes," she whispered. "That."

Abner Clay stopped by twice a day without fail.

First in the morning, usually with a grin and some new observation about the train.

"Well now, Doctor Belle," he said the first morning, leaning against the doorframe, "you look downright settled."

"I am settled," she replied, closing her book. "And suspicious."

He laughed. "You earned every bit of this seat."

"And I'm determined to enjoy it until the road interrupts again," she said dryly.

Abner shook his head. "If the road interrupts you again, it's because it recognizes authority."

Later that afternoon, he returned with news, always news.

"We'll be stoppin' a few hours today," he told her. "Small town. Just refuel, collect the mail, stretch legs. Folks can eat at the boardinghouse if they like."

Belle nodded. "Three hours?"

"About that."

She smiled. "Enough time for trouble."

Abner raised a brow. "You expectin' it?"

"No," she replied. "But the road has habits."

He laughed again, deep and easy. "If something happens, I know where to find you."

"You always do," she said gently.

The stop came later than expected.

The train slowed, steam hissing, wheels grinding against the rails as the small station came into view. A handful of buildings clustered together—general store, boardinghouse, stable. Wagons waited nearby, drivers leaning against wooden rails, hats pulled low against the sun.

Belle stepped down carefully, grateful for the stretch.

She had just begun to walk toward the boardinghouse when movement near the platform caught her attention.

A family disembarked together.

A Mexican husband and wife, hands linked. Three small children clinging nervously to skirts and trousers. The woman was visibly heavy with child—so pregnant that Belle's breath caught instinctively.

As soon as her feet touched the ground, the woman gasped sharply and cried out.

"No—no, not now," she moaned, clutching her belly.

Pain bent her nearly double.

The children began to cry.

The husband panicked. "María—mi amor—hold on—"

Two wagons stood waiting nearby.

The first driver, Joaquín Rivera, sprang forward immediately.
The second, Luis Ortega, followed close behind, faces tightening with concern.

"Get her down," Joaquín said urgently. "Careful."

María screamed again, grabbing at her husband's sleeve.

Belle was already moving.

"Doctor Belle!"

Abner Clay's voice cut through the noise as he ran from the train.

He didn't ask questions.

Didn't hesitate.

He grabbed her luggage and doctor's bag in one smooth motion and hauled them down from the car.

"I knew it," he muttered. "I just knew it."

Belle knelt beside the woman instantly.

"I'm a doctor," she said calmly, meeting María's eyes. "Look at me. We're going to take care of you."

María sobbed, breath hitching. "Dolor… mucho dolor…"

Belle switched gently, slowly.

"I understand. The pain is strong. How far is your home?"

The husband—Rafael Mendoza—answered quickly. "Five miles. Just five."

Belle nodded. "Then I'm coming with you."

Rafael stared at her. "You will?"

"Yes," she said firmly. "I'm a doctor."

Some passengers gathered closer, murmuring.

One refined woman from first class leaned down toward Belle, nose wrinkling.

"You should be careful," she whispered sharply. "You never know what diseases these people carry."

Belle did not even look at her.

She rose slightly and spoke clearly, so all could hear.

"Did not Jesus spit on the ground and make clay to heal the blind?" she asked calmly.
"Did He not touch lepers?"
"And yet virtue went out from Him."

186

She turned back to María.

"I am in good hands," Belle said softly. "And so are you."

They lifted María carefully into the wagon.

The children climbed in beside her, Rafael holding her hand, whispering prayers in Spanish.

As the wagons rolled forward, Belle climbed in as well.

The road stretched ahead.

Five miles.

Pain.

Prayer.

And a God who never seemed to mind interruptions.

The wagons creaked steadily along the dirt road, dust rising in soft clouds behind them as the small town disappeared from view. Belle sat beside María, one hand braced against the wagon's side and the other steadying the laboring woman as another pain tore through her body.

María cried out sharply, clutching her belly.

"Respira, mi amor," Rafael whispered, pressing his forehead to hers. "Respira conmigo."

Belle watched her breathing, watched the tension in her face, the way her body labored harder than it should have for a woman not yet at full term.

Something did not add up.

Five miles never felt so long.

When they crested a low rise, the village came into view.

It was small, tightly knit, and alive with motion. Adobe-style homes sat close together, their earth-toned walls warmed by the sun. Smoke rose from outdoor cooking hearths. Chickens darted freely between doorways. Children paused in their play as the wagons approached, eyes widening at the sight of María bent nearly double in pain.

"La comadrona!" someone shouted. "No—no es la comadrona—es doctora," another voice answered urgently.

The wagons rolled into the center of the village, stopping in front of a modest but well-kept home with a low porch and flowering herbs planted carefully along the edges. It was clear this was María and Rafael's home.

Hands appeared immediately.

Women came running, skirts gathered, shawls thrown hastily over shoulders. Older women moved faster than expected, authority in their posture. Younger women followed, eyes sharp, already prepared to serve.

"Despacio," Belle said gently as they lifted María down. "Slowly. Her body is under too much strain."

They carried her inside.

The home was simple but full of life.

Whitewashed walls reflected the light. Clay pots lined the shelves. Corn hung drying near the back door. A handwoven rug softened the packed-earth floor. Everything had its place, not from wealth, but from care.

They laid María on a wide bed layered with blankets and quilts stitched by many hands. The room filled quickly—perhaps too quickly—but Belle did not push them away.

Not yet.

She knelt at María's side, her voice calm, grounding.

"María, mírame," she said gently. "I need to examine you."

María nodded weakly, another contraction ripping through her with such force that she screamed, clutching Belle's forearm.

Belle's brow furrowed.

This pain was wrong.

Too early. Too intense. Too close together.

Belle examined her carefully, methodically, years of training settling into place.

Her breath caught.

"Oh my goodness," she whispered.

She looked up at Rafael.

"María is carrying three babies."

The room erupted.

"¿Tres?"
"¡Dios mío!"
"Three—three babies?"

189

María sobbed openly now, fear flooding her face.

"No… no sabía," she cried. "I didn't know."

Belle took her face gently in both hands.

"That is why you are so large. That is why the pain is so strong. Your body has been carrying more than one life—three lives—this entire time."

Rafael staggered back, bracing himself against the wall.

"Three," he breathed. "Señor Jesús…"

Belle straightened.

"We will need help," she said firmly. "Many hands. Clean cloth. Hot water—boiling. Food for strength. And prayer."

No one questioned her.

They moved instantly.

Women flooded the space with purpose.

Isabel Morales, older and sharp-eyed, took charge of water and cloths.
Rosa Delgado gathered herbs from the garden without needing direction.
Carmen Flores took the children outside and organized food.
Lucía Navarro, barely eighteen but steady as stone, stayed by Belle's side, watching every move.

Belle had never seen such unity.

Someone pressed warm bread into Rafael's hands.

"You must eat," Carmen said firmly. "You must be strong too."

Outside, men gathered wood. Inside, women prayed aloud, quietly, fiercely.

"Jesús…"
"Dios santo…"
"Virgen María—no—Jesús—Jesús…"

Belle noticed it immediately.

Their prayers flowed constantly—but Jesus' name surfaced naturally, without fear or formality.

That mattered.

The labor intensified.

María screamed, body arching, sweat soaking her hair.

"I can't," she sobbed. "No puedo. It hurts too much."

Belle leaned close.

"Yes, you can," she said firmly. "You were built for this. But you are not alone."

Another contraction tore through her.

Belle realized something else then.

María's body would not manage this without intervention.

"Jesús," Belle whispered under her breath. "Only You could pull off something like this."

She looked at the women.

"Listen to me," she said clearly. "These babies will come one at a time. We must not rush. We must guard her strength."

Isabel nodded. "We will do as you say."

They turned the room into organized calm amid chaos.

Hours passed.

The first baby came just after sunset.

A girl.

Small but strong, crying immediately.

"¡Una niña!" someone shouted joyfully.

They cleaned her quickly and placed her against María's chest.

María sobbed—not from pain now, but wonder.

"I hear her," she whispered. "Gracias, Jesús…"

Belle barely allowed herself a breath before preparing again.

The second labor began quickly.

Harder. More dangerous.

María shook uncontrollably.

"I'm tired," she whispered. "No more."

Belle leaned close, forehead pressed to hers.

"You are not finished," she said gently. "But God is not finished with you either."

The women prayed louder now.

"Jesús, Jesús, Jesús…"

The second baby arrived—a boy.

Silent at first.

Belle's heart slammed into her ribs.

She worked quickly, firm hands, whispered prayers.

"Breathe… come on… breathe…"

A weak cry emerged.

The room erupted again—this time with tears and praise.

"Gloria a Dios!"

But Belle's hands did not stop.

"There is still one more," she reminded them quietly.

Exhaustion nearly crushed María.

Belle felt it keenly.

"Everyone," she said softly, authority steady, "pray."

They obeyed.

Out loud. Together.

"Jesús, only You…"
"Jesús, strength…"
"Jesús, life…"

Belle felt it—an unmistakable presence settle over the room.

When the third baby came, it was as if hands unseen were guiding the process.

Another girl.

Smallest of the three.

But breathing.

Alive.

Belle sank back on her heels, tears finally spilling free.

"Three," she whispered. "All alive."

They fed Belle that night as though she were family.

Soup rich with vegetables. Fresh tortillas. Sweet tea infused with herbs meant for strength.

They gave her a small, quiet room to rest, clean linens scented with lavender and rosemary.

"You stay," Isabel said firmly. "You are one of us tonight."

Belle did not argue.

She lay awake later, listening to the village breathe.

Children laughing softly.
Babies nursing.
Women humming lullabies.

Togetherness pressed in on every side.

Before sleep took her, Belle whispered one last prayer.

"Jesus," she said quietly, "only You could do this. Only You."

In the corner of the room, someone had placed a small wooden carving—a simple cross, hands rough but reverent.

Belle smiled.

Tomorrow, they would tell her about the village.

And another chapter would begin.

CHAPTER EIGHTEEN

Belle woke before the sun, as she often did, to the sound of life asserting itself.

Not the orderly bustle of trains or the distant clang of bells—but the soft, human rhythm of a village beginning another day. A baby cried briefly and then settled. Someone laughed quietly outside. The low murmur of voices drifted through the thin walls of the home where Belle had been given rest.

She rose, wrapped her shawl around her shoulders, and washed her hands carefully. Habit, discipline, reverence—these things mattered most when life was newly arrived.

When she entered María's room, the air felt warmer, heavier with breath and tenderness.

María lay propped against pillows, her long dark hair braided loosely over one shoulder. Her face was pale but peaceful, eyes bright with exhaustion and awe. She was only thirty years old, but already the weight of responsibility rested in her posture.

"Buenos días, doctora," María whispered with a tired smile.

"Buenos días," Belle replied softly, returning the smile. "How do you feel?"

"Tired," María said honestly. "But alive."

Belle nodded approvingly. "That is an excellent place to begin."

She moved gently to the first cradle—a shallow wooden box lined with folded cloth.

"Let's see our firstborn," Belle said.

The little girl stirred as Belle lifted her carefully. She was small but strong, her fists already balled with determination. Her cry, when it came, was sharp and indignant—as if offended by the interruption.

"There's her voice," Belle murmured with satisfaction. "Strong lungs. Good color."

María's eyes followed every movement.

"She cries like Rafael," María said softly.

Belle smiled. "Then she will be heard."

She checked the baby's breathing, heart rate, fingers, toes—each detail a quiet confirmation of life. She returned her gently and moved to the second cradle.

The boy slept deeply, chest rising in steady rhythm. Belle checked him with extra care, remembering the frightening stillness when he had first arrived.

"You gave us quite the pause," Belle said quietly to him.

María's hand trembled slightly as she reached out to touch his blanket.

"I thought we lost him," María whispered.

"But you didn't," Belle replied. "He fought his way in."

She examined him thoroughly, nodding.

"He's strong. He will need frequent feeding—but his heart is good. His body wants to live."

Tears slid silently down María's cheeks.

Finally, Belle approached the third cradle.

The smallest.

The quietest.

The little girl slept curled in on herself, fragile and fierce all at once.

Belle bent close, her expression serious.

"You're the one I'll watch most carefully," she murmured.

She checked the baby thoroughly—temperature, breathing, reflex. The infant shifted and let out the faintest sound, barely a whimper.

"There," Belle said with relief. "That's enough."

María released a breath she didn't know she was holding.

"All three," she whispered. "Jesús…"

Belle turned back to María now.

"And you," she said gently. "How does your body feel?"

"Sore everywhere," María replied with a soft laugh. "Like I ran miles."

"You did," Belle said. "Inwardly."

She checked María carefully—pulse, abdomen, signs of infection or excessive bleeding.

"You must rest," Belle instructed firmly. "Your body carried three lives. You cannot rush healing."

María nodded obediently.

"I will do what you say."

That trust mattered.

Later in the morning, Belle stepped outside into full daylight.

The village revealed itself in greater detail now that she could see without urgency clouding her vision. Homes were close together—not cramped, but connected. People lived near one another deliberately, sharing labor and watchfulness.

Children played nearby, some tasked with gathering water, others watching younger siblings. Chickens wandered freely. A group of men worked together repairing a section of roof damaged by last season's storms.

Women prepared food in shared spaces—corn ground, beans simmered, bread baked communally.

They worked together because survival demanded it.

They thrived together because love sustained it.

Belle saw no excess—but no abandonment either.

It was near midday when Elena Morales approached her.

Elena was eighteen—barely more than a girl by some standards, yet already composed with purpose. Her hair was pulled back simply, eyes attentive and intelligent.

"Doctora," Elena said respectfully, "may I ask you something?"

"Of course," Belle replied.

Elena hesitated only a moment.

"I want to be like you," she said. "I want to learn healing. Medicine."

Belle studied her carefully—not dismissively, but discerningly.

"That is not a small desire," Belle said. "Why?"

Elena didn't answer immediately.

"When my little brother died," she said softly, "there was no one to help him. My mother held him while he burned with fever. We prayed, but we did not know what else to do."

Belle's chest tightened.

"So now," Elena continued, voice steady, "I want to know what else can be done."

Belle nodded slowly.

"There are schools," she said. "But they are few—and not welcoming to everyone."

Elena's shoulders fell slightly.

"Then how?" she asked.

Belle placed a hand over hers.

"Learning begins before schools," Belle said. "I will teach you what I can. Reading. Anatomy. Clean practice. Observation."

Elena's breath caught.

"You would?"

"Yes," Belle said firmly. "And if God opens a door to formal schooling, we will walk through it together."

Tears filled the young girl's eyes.

"No white doctor has ever spoken to us like this," Elena whispered.

Belle met her gaze steadily.

"No one is born less worthy of learning," she replied.

That evening, as the village gathered for shared supper, Belle watched quietly as families ate together. Children sat at the feet of elders. Stories were passed as naturally as bread.

She realized then what unsettled her most.

They were used to being unseen.

Not merely ignored—but dismissed.

And yet they had built something enduring anyway.

As the sun dipped low and voices softened, a man near the fire spoke quietly.

"She stays," he said to another. "She sees us."

Belle lowered her head slightly, humbled.

She whispered a prayer into the stillness.

"Lord, teach me how to honor them well."

Tomorrow, there would be questions they had never been allowed to ask.

And Belle would listen.

Belle did not sleep easily that night.

Not because the village was loud—it had settled into a familiar hush—but because her spirit would not rest.

Questions pressed in the quiet hours, not frantic ones, but steady, searching ones that refused to be ignored.

She rose before dawn and stepped outside, the ground cool beneath her feet. The sky was just beginning to soften from black to deep blue, stars slowly surrendering their hold.

Belle wrapped her shawl tighter and knelt.

"Jesus," she whispered, voice barely audible, "You did not bring me here only for the babies. You brought me here for the future. Show me what obedience looks like next."

She sat with Him for a long time.

Not asking for ideas.

Asking for clarity.

Later that morning, Belle gathered several of the young people beneath the shade of a large mesquite tree near the center of the village. They came hesitantly at first, unsure why she had asked to speak with them, then with increasing curiosity.

Elena Morales sat closest, eyes bright and alert.

Others joined—young men with callused hands, young women with infants tied to their backs, children hovering nearby pretending not to listen.

Belle spoke gently.

"I need to learn from you," she said. "Tell me—where do your children receive schooling?"

There was an uneasy pause.

A man named Mateo Cruz cleared his throat. "Sometimes… they do not."

Another woman, Ana Ruiz, answered quietly. "The older ones teach the younger when they can. Reading is rare. Writing even more so."

"Who teaches you your trades?" Belle asked.

"Our fathers," Mateo replied. "Our mothers. We learn by watching."

Belle nodded thoughtfully.

"And when you work outside the village?"

A murmur rippled through the group.

"They pay us less," one man said bluntly.
"They cheat us," another added. "Say we did not finish the work."
"If we argue, we are told to leave."

Belle's hands clenched quietly in her lap.

"You deserve fair wages," she said. "Every single time."

Ana looked down. "They say we should be grateful to have any work."

Belle inhaled slowly.

"And the railroad station?" she asked carefully. "Why do you not sell your goods there?"

Mateo laughed without humor.

"We tried. Once."

Another voice—Rafael, still weary from the long night—spoke up. "They told us we were not permitted. Said our carts made the place look disorderly."

"But other groups sell there," Belle said.

"Yes," Elena replied softly. "Just not us."

Silence settled heavily.

Belle let it.

Then she spoke again.

"What do you want for your children?" she asked.

The answers came faster now.

"To read."
"To write."
"To choose."
"To move west and buy land."
"To be safe."

"To not disappear."

That last one hung in the air.

Belle felt the shape of her calling shift.

Not abandoning her destination—

Expanding it.

She bowed her head again, even as she sat among them.

"Jesus," she prayed aloud this time, unashamed, "You hear them. You always have. Teach me how to help without taking over. Show us favor where doors have been shut."

She looked up.

"I cannot fix everything," she said honestly. "But I can write letters."

Hope flickered.

"To my medical school—Henry," she continued. "I will ask them to send not just a doctor, but teachers. People who understand medicine, mathematics, reading—people who respect your culture."

Elena leaned forward. "They would come here?"

"I will ask," Belle said. "And I will not stop asking."

"And will they listen?" Ana asked quietly.

"They listened once," Belle said. "I trust God with twice."

That afternoon, Belle sat at the small table inside María and Rafael's home, paper spread before her, words forming slowly but deliberately.

She wrote about the village.

About the babies.

About the hunger for learning.

About children who deserved more than survival.

About young women who wanted to become healers.

About men who labored honestly and were treated unfairly.

She also knew something else was missing.

They needed an advocate nearby.

205

Someone with standing.

Someone known.

"Lord," she whispered again, pen paused, "send a bridge."

She asked the people directly.

"Who in the nearby town treats you with fairness?" she asked later that evening.

There was hesitation.

Then Rafael spoke.

"There is a shopkeeper," he said. "Not rich. But kind. His name is Thomas Whitaker. He does not cheat."

Belle nodded. "That's a beginning."

She wrote his name down too.

When the prayers rose that night, they sounded different.

Not only gratitude.

Expectation.

Children gathered close, listening.

Elena sat beside Belle, watching every movement as if learning began simply by proximity.

Before sleep, Belle prayed one last time.

"Jesus," she said softly, "let education come without erasure. Let justice come with dignity. And let me move forward knowing You are already at work behind me."

Outside, the village settled.

Inside, something had shifted.

Not rescue.

Not charity.

Alignment.

And Belle knew—without doubt—

She would write many more letters before her journey ended.

But this one would matter for generations.

Chapter Eighteen

Belle asked the question gently, but directly.

"And the work—tell me what kind of work you do to feed your families."

At first, they answered cautiously, as if work itself had been used against them before.

Then Mateo Cruz spoke, his voice steady.

"We work the land when we can. Seasonal work. Harvesting beans, chilies, corn. We follow the seasons."

Ana Ruiz added, "The women weave. Blankets, rugs, shawls. We dye them ourselves. Indigo, cochineal, plant roots. Traders sell them for much more than we receive."

Several heads nodded.

Rafael spoke next. "Some of us raise goats and chickens. We sell eggs, cheese, milk. But when we take them to town, the price changes when they see us."

Belle felt a familiar tightening in her chest. Not anger alone—recognition.

"And skilled labor?" she asked.

A young man named Diego Alvarez lifted his hand slightly. "Carpentry. Wagons. Repairs. I learned from my father. He learned from his."

Another man, Santos Herrera, added, "Leatherwork. Saddles. Reins. Harnesses. Ranches depend on us. But they do not remember us when payment is due."

Elena spoke softly but firmly. "We cook. For ranches. For crews. For travelers. Our food is requested—then undervalued."

An older woman, Soledad Montoya, her hands worn but steady, said, "Midwifery. Healing herbs. We know plants. We know fevers. But they do not call it medicine when we do it."

That one made Belle inhale slowly.

"No," she said quietly. "They call it ignorance—until they need it."

Murmurs of agreement rippled through the group.

Belle looked around and saw what had been invisible to others but unmistakable to her:

They were farmers.
Artisans.
Midwives.
Carpenters.
Animal caretakers.
Cooks.
Merchants without stalls.

A functioning economy—kept deliberately outside the gates of legitimacy.

"And the railroad?" Belle asked again. "Do any of you work there?"

A few men nodded.

"Track maintenance," Mateo said. "Loading. Unloading. Hard labor. Dangerous work."

"And selling to passengers?" Belle pressed.

Rafael shook his head. "Not allowed."

Belle looked up toward the distant tracks, imagination already at work.

"You produce food," she said slowly. "You make textiles. Leather. Repairs. These are exactly the kinds of things railroad towns require."

Elena's eyes widened. "Then why—"

"Because permission has nothing to do with usefulness," Belle said. "It has to do with control."

She let that truth settle before continuing.

"You are not unskilled," she said firmly. "You are unacknowledged."

That sentence landed like a stone dropped in water.

"And education," Belle continued, "does not replace your work. It protects it. It teaches contracts, numbers, records, rights."

Ana whispered, "So they cannot cheat us."

"Yes," Belle said. "So they cannot pretend you do not know better."

Belle stood then, her voice calm but resolute.

"You have trades worth defending. Children worth teaching. Families worth sustaining. Wanting to sell openly, travel west, and buy land is not rebellion. It is stewardship."

They listened with their whole bodies.

"For now," Belle added honestly, "I am one voice. But I will write for others—doctors, teachers, advocates— people who speak your language and the language used against you."

She paused, then smiled gently.

"And in the meantime, I will teach what I know."

Elena swallowed hard. "Will you start tomorrow?"

Belle smiled wider.

"Yes," she said. "Tomorrow."

The village did not erupt. They did not cheer.

They simply breathed differently—as if someone had finally spoken aloud what they had always known to be true.

They were not lacking worth.

They were lacking access.

And Belle intended to address that—with letters, with teaching, with prayer, and with the kind of persistence only Jesus seemed to give.

CHAPTER NINETEEN

Belle woke up smiling.

It was the satisfied kind of smile that came from real sleep—not the light, half-alert rest she'd grown used to on trains and in temporary lodgings, but the deep, bone-level kind that only arrived when a place, however briefly, felt like home.

The air in María and Rafael's house smelled of corn, woodsmoke, and something herbal simmering slowly over the fire. Somewhere nearby, one of the babies let out a small cry, immediately answered by a soft shushing voice. Belle lay there for a moment, listening.

"Thank You, Jesus," she whispered. "Everyone is still breathing. That's a good start."

Then another thought settled in just as clearly.

You have work to do.

Not stitches and bandages.

Letters and bridges.

She sat up, swung her legs over the edge of the pallet, and bowed her head.

"Lord," she prayed quietly, "these people need more than my hands. They need direction. They need justice. They need connections I do not yet have—but You do. Show me where to step today."

A verse surfaced in her thoughts as if carried on the morning light.

"And I will restore to you the years that the locust hath eaten."

She smiled softly.

"Yes," she said. "Let's begin."

Breakfast was shared at a long, narrow table just outside the house. A few neighbors had drifted over— bringing food, laughter, and news as naturally as they brought themselves. Fresh tortillas wrapped in cloth. Beans cooked with onion and a hint of chilies. A small bowl of scrambled eggs, stretched carefully to feed as many as possible.

"Doctora, coma," Carmen urged, sliding a plate toward Belle. "You worked harder than all of us yesterday."

Belle chuckled. "My legs disagree. They say you did more."

Elena joined them, notebook clutched close.

"You're leaving today?" she asked, trying to sound casual and failing badly.

"Leaving this village?" Belle clarified. "Not immediately. I still have work to do here before I resume my journey."

Rafael came out, looking somewhat less like a man who had nearly fainted through the births yesterday.

"Work?" he repeated nervously. "More… babies?"

"Not today," Belle said kindly. "Today my work involves questions. And walking."

She took a sip of her tea, then turned to Elena.

"I need to speak to Mr. Whitaker in town," *(he was not related to the wealthy family from her previous stay)* she said. "Thomas Whitaker. You mentioned him yesterday."

Rafael nodded. "He is fair. As fair as a man can be with so many pressures."

"I want to ask him some things," Belle said. "About permits. Licenses. How this town actually functions when it comes to business and law."

213

Elena's eyes lit. "He will talk to you. He respects learning."

"And I respect honesty," Belle replied. "Sounds like a promising start."

An hour later, Belle found herself perched in a small wagon beside Elena, rattling along a dusty road that connected the village to the nearby town. The ride was bumpy enough to keep them from getting too serious.

"So," Belle said, gripping the side of the seat as they hit a rut, "tell me what I'm walking into."

Elena smiled wryly. "A town that believes it is generous because it is not openly cruel."

"That," Belle said, "is one of the sharpest descriptions I've heard in a while."

"There are kind people," Elena continued. "But they are… quiet. They don't know how to speak against the others."

"Then we will give them something to agree with," Belle replied. "Quietly, at first."

The town appeared ahead—small but structured, with a main street lined by familiar buildings: general store, livery stable, boardinghouse, a small church, and the low, spreading shape of the railroad depot off to one side.

"Which one is Mr. Whitaker's shop?" Belle asked.

Elena pointed to a two-story building with clean windows and a freshly painted sign.

"Whitaker's Mercantile," it read. "Supplies, Dry Goods, Fair Weights."

Belle smiled. "Fair weights. That's promising."

Thomas Whitaker was behind the counter when they entered, sleeves rolled up, spectacles perched halfway down his nose. He was neither young nor old—somewhere in that middle stretch where people either hardened or softened. He appeared to have chosen soft.

He glanced up, saw Elena first, and smiled.

"Miss Morales," he said. "You don't often come in this early."

Elena stepped aside. "Mr. Whitaker, this is Doctora Belle. She helped María Mendoza. With the babies."

Something flickered in his eyes.

"I heard," he said. "Three of them, wasn't it?"

"Yes," Belle replied. "And everyone is alive. Only Jesus could have pulled that off. I just tried not to interfere."

Whitaker chuckled. "Modesty and accuracy in the same sentence. Uncommon combination."

Belle approached the counter.

"Mr. Whitaker," she said, extending her hand. "I need your help. Or at least your knowledge."

He shook her hand firmly.

"Well now," he replied, "those are two things I can sometimes provide. What are you after?"

215

"Information first," Belle said. "Influence later."

He laughed. "Careful. That sounds like planning."

"It is," she admitted. "For the village nearby. The one everyone uses for labor and forgets when the work is done."

His expression sobered.

"You've seen that already?" he asked quietly.

"Yesterday," she replied. "And the day before that. It doesn't take long."

He leaned his elbows on the counter.

"All right then," he said. "Ask your questions."

Belle didn't waste time.

"How does a person—or a group—get permission to sell at the railroad station?" she asked. "Food, goods, crafts."

Whitaker snorted softly.

"In theory? They apply for a vendor's license with the town council and the rail agent. In practice? The rail agent picks who he's comfortable with, and the council rarely argues."

"And who is the rail agent?" Belle asked.

"Edward P. Collins," Whitaker said. "Thin man. Expensive hat. Doesn't tolerate dust on his boots or strangers in his schedule."

"Charming," Belle murmured. "And the council?"

"Four men," Whitaker said. "Mayor Turner, two shop owners, and a rancher who thinks every person with brown skin is trespassing."

Belle held his gaze. "And yet you…"

"I sell them all things," Whitaker replied. "And I weigh those things fairly, whether they like it or not."

She nodded once. "That's a form of resistance."

"Some days it feels like my only one," he admitted.

She moved to her next question.

"If someone works a job and is not paid fully—or at all—where do they go?"

Whitaker sighed.

"Officially? The sheriff."

Belle raised a brow. "And unofficially?"

"They go home," he said. "Or they yell, get threatened, and then go home."

"No one presses charges?" Belle asked.

"Pressing charges requires believing you'll be heard," he said quietly. "Many of them have learned otherwise."

She nodded slowly.

"What about food permits?" she continued. "For rallies. Town events. Revivals. Who grants permission to sell there?"

"That would be the mayor," Whitaker said. "Or the church deacons if it's on church grounds. And they prefer to keep things… respectable."

"By which they mean familiar," Belle said.

"Exactly," he agreed.

Belle paused.

"And the young women?" she asked softly. "I've heard whispers of… misuse. Children from situations that began as work and ended as harm."

Whitaker's jaw tightened.

"Yes," he said. "That happens. Too often. Men from town, ranches, sometimes even travelers. The girls come to work—cleaning, cooking—and leave with reputations they did not ask for and babies they did not plan for."

"And what protection exists for them?" Belle asked.

He looked almost embarrassed.

"None that's written down," he said. "Sometimes I warn them when I can. Sometimes I refuse to extend credit to men who treat them badly. But that's a thin wall against a strong river."

Belle exhaled slowly.

"All right," she said. "Then here's what I'm thinking."

Whitaker's brows rose.

"I'm listening."

"First," Belle said, ticking points off on her fingers, "I will write to my medical school—Henry. Ask them to send a doctor. And teachers. People willing to live in that village or near it."

Whitaker nodded slowly. "That would make a difference."

"Second," Belle continued, "I will write to a wealthy family I recently helped. Their son nearly died. They have influence, and they know how to use it. I will ask them to put pressure on the railway company itself regarding vendor access at this station."

"You think they'd bother with a town this small?" Whitaker asked.

"They will if I ask in the right way," Belle said. "God did not give them connections only for social events."

Whitaker chuckled. "I'd like to see their faces when they read that."

"Third," Belle went on, "I want to petition—for the village—to obtain vendor licenses. In their names. For selling at the station and at town gatherings. Official, signed, stamped. Harder to ignore."

Whitaker tapped the counter thoughtfully.

"You'll need someone to bring those petitions into the right rooms," he said. "Someone who isn't turned away at the door."

Belle met his eyes.

"I was hoping you might be that someone," she said.

He stared at her for a moment, then sighed.

"Well," he said, "I do have decent handwriting."

Belle smiled. "And a conscience."

"That too," he admitted.

She leaned in.

"What forms do I need?" she asked. "What signatures? What language makes powerful men feel like this was their idea?"

Whitaker chuckled, but there was respect in it.

"You don't think small, do you, Doctor Belle?"

"I don't pray small," she replied. "The rest tends to follow."

He reached under the counter and pulled out a small stack of papers.

"These are the vendor forms," he said. "Unused. Because nobody's bothered to hand them to the right people."

Belle accepted them.

"And for events?" she asked.

"Write directly to Mayor Turner," Whitaker said. "Use words like 'respectability,' 'order,' and 'community goodwill.' Those are his weak spots."

"And the girls?" Belle asked quietly. "Protection. If we can't change hearts overnight, we can certainly change habits."

Whitaker sighed.

"If a sheriff took their cases seriously," he said, "that would shift things. But our sheriff is… cautious."

"Then perhaps," Belle said, "your sheriff needs to receive a letter as well. From another sheriff. One who married a nurse."

Whitaker gave her a long, curious look.

"You," he said slowly, "are more connected than you appear, Doctor Belle."

"Jesus is," she replied. "I'm just keeping up."

Before she left the shop, Belle asked one more question.

"Will you stand with them?" she asked plainly. "Not just with your scales and prices—but with your voice? When the petitions come?"

Whitaker considered that for a long moment.

Then he nodded, firmly.

"Yes," he said. "I will."

"Why?" she asked.

He smiled faintly.

"Because I'd like to meet my Maker someday with something better to say than, 'I kept the shelves tidy.'"

Belle laughed softly.

"That," she said, "is the best answer I've heard all week."

As she and Elena climbed back into the wagon to return to the village, Belle clutched the papers in her hands like seeds.

"Now we pray over these," she said.

Elena glanced sideways. "Over… papers?"

"Over everything," Belle replied. "If we expect justice to grow from this, the soil must be soaked in prayer first."

She bowed her head right there in the wagon as it lurched forward.

"Lord," she said aloud, "You hear the cries of the oppressed. You see the unpaid, the unseen, the unheard. Take these petitions, these forms, these names—and breathe on them. Turn injustice into justice. Turn indifference into intervention. And let no one be able to say they did not know."

When she opened her eyes, Elena was staring at her.

"What?" Belle asked gently.

"I think," Elena said, "you are more dangerous than any sheriff."

Belle smiled.

"I certainly hope so," she replied.

The village waited ahead.

Letters waited to be written.

And God, Belle suspected, was already several steps ahead of her.

Belle sharpened her pencil and smiled.

"Well," she said to no one in particular, "if I'm going to make a nuisance of myself for the Kingdom, I might as well do it thoroughly."

She had claimed one corner of Whitaker's store for the afternoon—Thomas had cleared a small table near the window and declared it temporary official business. He had even offered ink, envelopes, and the use of his mailing address, shaking his head with a half-smile as he did so.

"Seems safer," he said. "People read things more carefully when they come from here."

"Exactly," Belle replied. "Respectable paper has a way of getting past closed doors."

She wrote the return address neatly:

c/o Whitaker's Mercantile
Main Street

Then she began.

The first letter was to Henry.

She chose her words carefully—firm, respectful, and unignorable.

She wrote of a village with no formal schooling, of skilled workers without protection, of women desperate for medical care and children hungry for learning. She asked— not politely, but purposefully—for a doctor willing to live among them, and for teachers who spoke Spanish and understood community-based education.

She paused mid-sentence, then added:

These are not people in need of saving. They are people in need of partnership.

Belle underlined the sentence once, nodded, and continued.

The second letter went to the wealthy family—the ones who still wrote her Christmas cards and whose son still walked, laughed, and climbed trees because God had intervened when she'd been present.

She reminded them gently of that fact.

Then she asked.

She asked them to contact the railroad officials they knew. She asked them to speak of vendor access, fairness, and decency as if it were their own idea—which, she knew, would work better.

She ended the letter with Scripture.

"To whom much is given, much is required."

"Yes," she murmured. "That should do."

She sealed each letter carefully and stacked them beside her elbow.

Thomas Whitaker passed by, glanced down, and whistled softly.

"How many saints are you stirring up today?" he asked.

"Enough," Belle replied. "Hopefully."

Life in the village did not stop while ink dried.

María met Belle each morning now, babies bundled securely across her chest, eyes brighter every day.

"They slept three hours in a row," María announced one morning, voice awed. "I thought something had gone wrong."

Belle laughed. "That's what rest feels like. It's alarming the first time."

She checked each baby carefully—weight, temperature, breathing.

The first girl remained fierce and loud.
The boy was sturdier by the day.
The smallest girl still demanded extra care, but her color was improving, her strength growing.

"You are doing beautifully," Belle told María honestly.

"I eat," María said proudly. "When you say."

"Good," Belle replied. "Healing requires cooperation."

María nodded, then hesitated.

"You stay?" she asked quietly.

"For now," Belle said. "Long enough to set some things in motion."

In the late afternoons, Belle gathered the young women.

Not formally. Not rigidly.

They came because they trusted her.

They sat together—some sewing, some holding children, some listening more than speaking.

Belle spoke plainly.

"It is not safe," she said gently, "for you to go alone to ranches or into town to cook and clean."

A murmur rose.

"That work feeds us," one woman said.

225

"I know," Belle replied. "But without protection, it costs too much."

Another woman crossed her arms. "What choice do we have?"

Belle met her eyes steadily.

"You have one," she said. "Refuse."

Silence followed.

"Say no?" Elena asked carefully.

"Yes," Belle replied. "If someone wants food prepared, it must be done here. In the village."

"And delivery?" another woman asked.

"The men will deliver," Belle said simply. "Together. No lone girls. No isolated houses."

One woman snorted quietly. "They will not like that."

"Change rarely is," Belle replied.

They laughed—nervous, thoughtful laughter.

"And if they refuse?" another asked.

"Then you refuse too," Belle said. "Collectively."

She leaned forward.

"You are not weak because you need money. You are strong because you can choose how to earn it."

That landed.

Later, Belle noticed the children again—their variety unmistakable now that she knew what to look for.

A little girl with copper-red curls.
A boy with eyes startlingly blue.
Blond hair mixed among dark curls.

Each loved. Each cherished. Each conceived in circumstances that had not honored their mothers.

Belle felt the weight of it keenly.

She addressed the parents openly that evening.

"Our children carry many stories," she said. "Some painful. Some unjust. But they must not carry shame that does not belong to them."

Heads nodded slowly.

"Protection begins at home," Belle continued. "It is not enough to say men should behave better. We must arrange life so harm has fewer opportunities."

Someone spoke from the back. "What about food?"

Belle smiled slightly.

"You grow more than you think," she said. "If you pool labor and share land, you can survive among yourselves while change catches up."

That sparked conversation immediately—plots discussed, crops rotated, collective labor planned.

"It will be hard," a man said.

"Yes," Belle agreed cheerfully. "Hard is not the same as impossible."

That made them laugh.

She gave them rules—not commandments, but frameworks.

No young woman enters town alone.
No work that isolates without witnesses.
All decisions prayed over before action.
No shame allowed to linger unchallenged.

"And," she added lightly, "any man who objects too loudly likely knows exactly why."

That brought laughter—real, relieved laughter.

They prayed together before ending the meeting.

Not rushed. Not rehearsed.

"Jesús," one woman prayed. "Teach us courage."

Another whispered, "Teach us patience."

A man added, "Teach us to stand together."

Belle closed.

"Teach us wisdom before urgency."

That night, Belle sat again with her letters, now ready for posting.

Elena delivered the letters the next day to Thomas Whitaker who himself walked them to the outgoing mail sack.

"She is making trouble," he said mildly.

"Good trouble," Elena replied.

He nodded. "The kind that lasts."

Before bed, Belle opened her Bible one last time.

"Let us not be weary in well doing: for in due season we shall reap, if we faint not."

She smiled.

"I don't plan on fainting," she told the Lord.

Outside, the village settled into rest—not because its problems were solved, but because they were finally being addressed.

And Belle knew the next chapter would require even more courage.

CHAPTER TWENTY

It had been two months since Belle had arrived in the village—and for the first time in her life, staying felt just as purposeful as traveling.

Time had changed everything.

The babies were no longer the fragile bundles she had once hovered over with bated breath. They had grown sturdy and alert, their cries distinct now—three voices instead of one blended worry. The first girl had filled out, her cheeks round and expressive, her cry the loudest of the three, announcing her opinions on hunger and discomfort without hesitation. The boy had become solid, his limbs strong, his grip surprisingly firm when Belle placed her finger in his palm. The smallest girl, once watched so carefully, now breathed easily, her tiny chest rising with growing confidence, eyes bright and observant as if she were studying the world that had nearly slipped past her.

Belle smiled every time she checked them.

"They're thriving," she told María one morning, gently weighing the smallest. "Not just surviving. Thriving."

María herself had changed just as much.

Where once she had moved cautiously, guarding her body after the ordeal of birth, she now walked with renewed strength. Her color had returned, her posture straightened, her laughter easier. She worked again—not all day, not without rest—but with a pride that came from healing done properly.

"I feel strong again," María said, rolling her shoulders as they stood outside in the sun. "Like my body remembers itself."

"That," Belle replied, smiling, "is what healing feels like when it's respected."

María laughed. "I like this kind better than surviving."

The biggest change, though, had come in the form of letters.

A letter came to the store. Belle held the one from Henry carefully the first time she opened it, her hands steady but her heart racing just the same.

She read it aloud to the small group gathered around her—Elena, Rafael, María, and several elders after she came back to the village.

We have received your letter and taken it seriously.

Belle paused, smiled faintly, and continued.

While we cannot immediately deploy a full staff, we anticipate that within four months—upon the next graduating class—we may be able to send a small team willing to serve in the capacity you described.

Gasps and whispers followed.

"But," Belle continued, lifting a finger, "listen to this part."

In the meantime, we are exploring the possibility of sending one physician and one educator sooner, should the appropriate arrangements be made.

Silence followed that.

Then Elena whispered, "They are coming?"

"Yes," Belle said softly. "They are trying."

María's hands flew to her mouth. "Jesús…"

An older man cleared his throat. "They did not laugh?"

"No," Belle replied. "They listened."

The reaction spread slowly, deeply.

Not celebration yet.

Hope—with caution.

"They have not forgotten us," someone said in disbelief.

"No," Belle answered gently. "And you will not let them regret remembering."

That night, prayers sounded different again.

Less pleading.

More expectation.

Another letter arrived two weeks later—this one bearing the unmistakable seal of the railroad authority.

Belle gathered everyone again.

She read slowly.

The railway grants permission for one village-operated wagon to sell goods and food at the station on days when trains arrive. This privilege is extended under company authority and is not subject to local interference.

A stunned pause followed.

Then she continued.

Local authorities are instructed not to obstruct this arrangement. Failure to comply may result in fines or revocation of station privileges.

The reaction was immediate and explosive.

The village erupted—not in shouting, but stunned disbelief, laughter mixed with tears, hands clasping hands.

"One wagon," Rafael said slowly. "One wagon change everything."

Outside the village, the reaction was less holy.

Locals were furious.

"You mean they get to sell and we don't get another license?" one regular vendor snapped.

"It isn't fair," another complained. "They'll undercut us."

But the railroad owned the land.

And the railroad had spoken.

When one vendor tried to argue with a station attendant, the man cut him off sharply.

"You interfere," he said flatly, "and you interfere with the railroad. We fine people for that."

That ended the discussion.

The village, meanwhile, prepared with trembling hands and steady resolve.

The morning the wagon first rolled into place, Belle stood beside it.

She insisted.

233

"I want to see it," she said simply.

The wagon itself was modest—painted clean, goods arranged carefully. Baskets of produce, bundles of woven blankets, hand-tooled leather goods, jars of preserved vegetables, fresh bread wrapped in cloth.

Elena adjusted the display nervously.

"What if no one comes?" she whispered.

Belle smiled calmly. "Trains bring hunger with them."

The train pulled in.

Steam hissed.

Passengers disembarked.

Then someone stopped.

Then another.

Soon, coins exchanged hands.

A woman purchased bread and smiled in surprise. "This is wonderful."

A man held up a woven shawl. "Who made this?"

"We did," Elena answered proudly.

Belle watched from just behind the wagon, hands clasped, heart pounding.

A regular vendor scowled from across the platform.

But when he started forward, a railroad attendant stepped into his path.

"Mind your business," the man said. "This is sanctioned."

That was it.

The wagon sold out before the last passenger reboarded.

When the train pulled away, the villagers stared at the empty shelves in disbelief.

"We sold everything," María whispered.

Belle laughed—soft, amazed laughter.

"Yes," she said. "You did."

They prayed right there, hands joined, ignoring the looks.

"Thank You, Jesus," someone said simply.

Belle added quietly, "For justice that shows up looking like opportunity."

She wiped her eyes and smiled wider.

Part One of the miracle was complete.

And everyone sensed it:

This was only the beginning.

The village did not sleep the night after the first wagon sold out.

They tried.

They truly did.

But joy has a way of pacing.

People sat outside their homes longer than usual, replaying the day again and again as if afraid it might disappear if not remembered in detail. Children mimicked

235

selling bread, waving imaginary coins and laughing. Older men spoke in low, astonished voices, counting and recounting figures that still did not seem real.

"For the first time," Rafael said quietly, seated beside the fire, "we were not hiding."

"No," Belle agreed. "You were authorized."

That word alone changed how people stood the next morning.

The second train day arrived with far less trembling.

The same wagon rolled forward, but this time with confidence. Goods were arranged more boldly. Signs—handwritten but clear—were placed where travelers could see.

Fresh Bread
Handwoven Goods
Farm Produce

Elena adjusted one sign, then looked at Belle.

"I didn't think ink on paper could feel this powerful," she said.

Belle smiled. "That's what legitimacy feels like."

The miracles that day were quieter—but no less real.

An elderly passenger purchased vegetables and remarked, "These look like my mother's garden."

A railway engineer returned twice for bread.

A woman who had passed the wagon the day before brought her friend specifically to buy shawls.

By midday, laughter replaced nervous whispers.

Not everyone rejoiced.

Across the platform, the regular vendors gathered in tight knots, watching with narrowed eyes.

"They're taking business," one hissed.

"They shouldn't even be here," another muttered.

One man stepped forward, fists clenched.

Before Belle could speak, a railroad attendant—Mr. Harris, his name stitched neatly on his vest—stepped in calmly.

"This wagon is protected under railway authority," he said plainly. "You interfere, you answer to us."

The man scoffed. "Since when does the railroad care about villagers?"

Mr. Harris didn't raise his voice.

"Since today," he said. "And since tomorrow. Now move."

That ended it.

The vendors backed away, grumbling but restrained.

Elena exhaled shakily. "I thought we were about to lose everything."

Belle shook her head. "No. The paperwork did its job."

That afternoon, Belle led the village in prayer—not hurried, not whispered.

They stood together behind the wagon, hands linked, voices unified.

"Thank You, Jesus," María prayed, her voice steady. "For dignity," another added.
"For provision," said an elder.
"For protection," Elena finished.

Belle closed gently.

"For wisdom, Lord, to steward this blessing without fear."

People passing by noticed.

Some stared.

Others bowed their heads quietly as they walked.

By the end of the second week, patterns formed.

The wagon sold out regularly.

Money was counted together.

Records were kept.

They discussed savings, reinvestment, seed purchases.

"This is business," Rafael said one evening, half-amazed. "Real business."

"It always was," Belle replied. "It simply lacked recognition."

And miracles continued—smaller, no less sacred.

A sick child recovered after proper nutrition.

A debt was quietly paid.

A baby learned to laugh.

The railroad letters kept coming.

Short confirmations.
Clear boundaries.
Unexpected firmness in the village's favor.

Local authorities learned not to argue.

The mayor avoided the subject entirely.

Silence became agreement.

For the first time, the village existed publicly without apology.

Belle watched it all carefully—rejoicing, teaching, correcting when needed.

She reminded them gently:

"This door stays open because you walk through it with order and respect."

They listened.

And changed.

That night, Belle knelt alone again.

"Jesus," she whispered, "thank You for justice that didn't arrive loud—but arrived lasting."

She rose knowing her destination still waited.

But now—

So did something else.

A people standing taller.

A future outlined

CHAPTER TWENTY

Belle knew she was supposed to leave.

The destination she had once spoken of with certainty still waited somewhere westward, patient but unmoved. Her trunk remained packed. Her letters of introduction stayed folded neatly in her bag. The train schedules were known to her by heart.

And yet—she stayed.

Not out of confusion.

Out of discernment.

"Two more months," she told the village elders quietly one evening. "I will stay two more months. If Henry sends help, it will happen in that time."

"If they do not?" Rafael asked gently.

Belle smiled. "Then we will know God intends another path."

No one argued.

By then, the village trusted not only Belle's hands—but her listening.

The days settled into a new rhythm.

Mornings were divided between teaching—basic reading, numbers, hygiene—and tending to the babies and elderly. Afternoons belonged to food preparation and goods production. Train days were communal events now, less frantic, more ordered.

The single sanctioned wagon stood proudly at the platform, its presence no longer tentative.

Money was counted carefully.

Ledgers were kept.

Decisions were made together.

Two months began to pass.

Then three months passed.

And on an ordinary train day—ordinary enough that no one expected anything more than sales—the extraordinary arrived.

The train pulled in just after midmorning, steam hissing as usual, metal groaning as it came to rest. Passengers disembarked lazily, stretching their legs, consulting watches, scanning the platform for food and shade.

Belle stood near the wagon, helping Elena arrange baskets of bread.

That was when she saw them.

An older gentleman—early forties, perhaps—with a neatly trimmed mustache and the posture of someone accustomed to being listened to. Beside him stood two young women in their twenties, composed, confident, dressed practically but well. All three wore traveling coats suited for professionals, not tourists.

They did not look lost.

They looked intentional.

241

The man scanned the platform, then approached the wagon.

He switched easily into Spanish.

"Disculpe," he said politely to Elena. "¿Conocen a la Doctora Belle?"

Elena froze.

Belle straightened slowly.

The question landed like a held breath released.

"Yes," Elena said carefully. "We know her."

The man smiled faintly. "Is she here?"

Elena turned, pointed, and said simply, "Esta es ella."

Belle felt the weight of the moment before she moved.

She stepped forward.

"I am Belle," she said. "May I help you?"

The man's smile widened.

"Yes," he said warmly. "You already have."

Introductions unfolded right there on the platform, between sacks of produce and the lingering heat of the train engine.

"I am Dr. Mateo Alvarez," the man said. "Physician."

He gestured to the woman at his right.

"This is Nurse Clara Johnson."

Clara nodded warmly—Black, poised, her eyes kind and observant.

"And this is Nurse Elizabeth Hartwell," he continued. "Elizabeth."

Elizabeth smiled—white, steady, with the calm presence of someone who had learned compassion through discipline rather than sentiment.

All three spoke Spanish fluently.

All three were well dressed.

All three were unmistakably professionals.

Belle's throat tightened.

"You came," she said softly.

Dr. Alvarez nodded. "We were… redirected sooner than expected."

Behind Belle, the village had gone utterly still.

They knew.

No one shouted.

No one rushed forward.

This was the crew they had prayed for.

Not announced.

Not heralded.

Delivered.

The train whistle blew.

Passengers reboarded.

The doors slammed shut.

And just like that, the train moved on—leaving behind four people who stood on the platform, staring at one another with the shared understanding that something irreversible had just occurred.

After a moment, Rafael spoke.

"Do you need a place to sit?" he asked politely, though his voice trembled.

Belle found her voice again.

"Yes," she said. "Yes, we do."

They led them away from the platform—not hurriedly, not ceremonially, but purposefully.

As they walked, Belle explained.

"We built housing," she said. "Small. Separate. It was important."

Dr. Alvarez's brows lifted. "You built houses?"

"With the profits," Elena said, unable to keep the pride from her voice. "From the wagon."

Clara stopped walking.

"You paid for them?" she asked.

"Yes," María said. "And we planned to provide room and board. And a small allowance. We know it is not much."

Dr. Alvarez looked genuinely moved.

"This," he said quietly, "is more than we were promised."

After riding several miles, they reached the edge of the village as the midday sun hung overhead.

There, tucked neatly beside one another, stood three modest but sturdy dwellings—freshly whitewashed, roofs sound, doors newly hung.

One for the doctor.

One for each nurse.

Belle stopped.

"We hoped you would come," she said honestly. "But we did not presume."

Elizabeth swallowed.

"I have never," she said softly, "been welcomed like this before."

Clara reached out and took María's hand.

"We are honored," she said.

No one spoke for a long moment.

Then Belle said what needed to be said.

"Welcome."

The village exhaled.

And somewhere beneath the sound of commerce, prayer, and iron rails, a foundation settled—quietly, firmly—into place.

They gathered that evening beneath the open sky.

Lanterns were hung carefully along the central gathering area, their light warm and steady, reflecting off faces that had learned—over time—to hope without demanding proof. Food appeared from every direction. Bread, beans, roasted vegetables, fresh cheese, stews simmered slowly, and sweets saved for special occasions.

This was a special occasion.

The village had learned not to rush such moments.

Dr. Mateo Alvarez stood near the fire first, clearing his throat with visible humility.

"I suppose," he said in Spanish, "that I should begin by explaining who I am and how I arrived here."

A few people smiled gently. Some children sat cross-legged at his feet. The older men folded their arms and listened carefully.

"I was born in San Antonio," Dr. Alvarez continued. "To Mexican parents who believed education was holy work. My mother was a midwife. My father a schoolteacher. I learned early that healing and learning travel together."

That earned approving nods.

"I attended medical school later than most," he went on. "I worked farms. Rail yards. Kitchens. Anything that would pay for one more book, one more term. I specialize in internal medicine, infections, and public health."

A murmur rose at that—people repeating the words quietly, testing them like new tools.

"When I received Belle's letter," he admitted, glancing toward her with warmth, "I could not put it down. Not because it was eloquent—but because it was honest."

That made Belle smile.

"She did not describe a desperate people," he said. "She described a capable one that had been denied opportunity."

Someone murmured, "Sí."

"I am single," Dr. Alvarez added frankly, prompting a ripple of gentle laughter. "And I go where God assigns me, not where comfort invites me."

That laughter softened into respect.

Nurse Clara Johnson stepped forward next.

She stood tall, graceful, her presence firm without needing volume.

"I am Clara," she said. "I was born in Louisiana. I trained as a nurse where people expected me to work twice as hard to be believed half as much."

Several women nodded knowingly.

"I learned obstetrics, children's care, and trauma medicine," Clara continued. "I have worked in cities, plantations, and places that had no names—only needs."

Her voice softened.

"I speak Spanish because my patients needed me to. I am colored. I am educated. I am faithful. And I am tired of being told where I do not belong."

A hush followed that—deep, reverent.

"When Henry asked if I would come," she said quietly, "I said yes because I recognized what was happening here."

She gestured gently to the village.

"You built room before we arrived."

That mattered.

Elizabeth Hartwell went last.

She smiled nervously at first—then steadied.

"I'm Elizabeth," she said. "I come from a family that believes good intentions excuse silence. I learned otherwise."

A few quiet chuckles greeted that.

"I trained in nursing because obedience without compassion frightened me," Elizabeth continued. "I wanted to know how to do something when prayer needed hands."

She paused.

"When this posting was offered, people warned me. They asked why I would go somewhere with no prestige and no guarantee."

Her eyes moved around the circle.

"I told them prestige does not heal. And neither does comfort."

That earned applause—genuine, warm applause.

The professionals were welcomed fully that night.

Not cautiously.

Not provisionally.

Children tested their names. Elders asked questions. Laughter came easily. Respect followed naturally.

Homes were visited. Supplies unpacked. Schedules discussed.

Plans formed.

And Belle watched it all quietly from the edge.

Satisfied.

Later—when the crowd thinned, and the lanterns burned lower—Belle stood.

The laughter faded slowly.

"I need to say something," she began.

Groans followed.

"No," someone said. "Doctora, no speeches."

Belle laughed softly. "I promise this one is short."

She looked around.

"You are no longer waiting," she said gently. "You are building."

Dr. Alvarez nodded. Clara and Elizabeth stood close, attentive.

"My staying was never meant to be permanent," Belle continued. "Only long enough for roots to take."

Elena's eyes widened.

"You're leaving?" she asked quietly.

Belle reached for her hand.

"Yes," she said. "It's time."

Silence pressed in now—thick, reluctant.

"You came to us," María said softly. "You stayed."

Belle smiled. "And now I go—knowing you are not alone."

She laughed gently. "Besides, someone out west has been waiting rather patiently for me to arrive."

That earned a few chuckles.

Dr. Alvarez stepped forward. "You laid this foundation," he said firmly.

Belle shook her head. "No. I recognized it."

She bowed her head.

"Jesus," she prayed aloud, voice steady but full, "thank You for ordering steps better than we could. Thank You for making room before sending help. Bless this village. Bless their work. Bless these professionals who said yes. And if I have done anything right here—let it continue long after I am gone."

Soft amens followed.

Some laughter came through tears.

Clara hugged Belle tightly. Elizabeth did the same.

"This is not goodbye," Clara said.

As Belle walked back toward her small room that night, heart full and eyes damp, she knew the truth plainly.

She had not been delayed.

She had been deployed.

And now—released.

CHAPTER TWENTY-ONE

Belle gathered them early the next morning, before the heat settled and before the railroad timetable tugged the village into motion.

Dr. Mateo Alvarez arrived first, coat neatly pressed, notebook in hand. Clara Johnson followed, already asking questions about supplies and schedules. Elizabeth Hartwell came last, calm and observant, her eyes catching details Belle had learned to trust.

"Thank you for coming," Belle said, motioning for them to sit on the low benches under the mesquite tree. "Today I want you to see the village at work—where faith became income."

Mateo smiled. "I've been told not to underestimate that wagon."

"Good," Belle replied. "Because it feeds families."

She spoke plainly, the way she always did when trust mattered.

"The railroad station is the village's main source of income right now. One sanctioned wagon. One chance each train day to turn labor into provision. I want you to see the town, the vendors, the railroad staff—and understand why protection, order, and relationships matter."

Elizabeth nodded. "You're thinking ahead."

"Yes," Belle said. "Which brings me to you, Elizabeth."

Elizabeth looked up, surprised but attentive.

"I want you to take my place," Belle continued. "Oversee the wagon. Work with the railroad staff. Keep records. Make sure nothing interferes with their right to sell. This single wagon is their livelihood."

Elizabeth drew in a breath. "That's… a great responsibility."

Belle smiled. "You are capable. And you will be fair."

Clara grinned. "That sounds like a promotion."

Elizabeth laughed softly. "I suppose it does."

The platform was already stirring when they arrived.

Railroad staff nodded to Belle with familiarity now. Mr. Harris tipped his hat politely.

"Morning, Doctor," he said. "Wagon's authorized as usual."

Elizabeth watched carefully as Belle greeted him, exchanged a few practical words, and moved on.

"That relationship," Belle said quietly to Elizabeth, "keeps everything calm."

Elizabeth nodded. "I see it."

As the wagon opened, townspeople drifted closer—curiosity tugging them in. Word had spread quickly.

"They've got their own doctor now," someone whispered.

"And a nurse," another added.

"I heard there's a colored nurse and a white one," a woman said, scandalized and intrigued.

A man scoffed. "Mexicans getting proud, if you ask me."

Belle heard it all. She didn't interrupt.

She introduced.

Dr. Mateo stood beside the wagon and spoke warmly with customers, explaining produce and herbs in Spanish and English alike. Clara offered guidance to a woman asking about a child's rash. Elizabeth kept notes, spoke with Mr. Harris, and gently redirected a regular vendor who edged too close.

"Authorized," Elizabeth said calmly, showing the letter. "Railroad rules."

The man backed off, muttering.

Belle leaned in. "Perfect."

The town noticed more than ethnicity.

They noticed competence.

They noticed order.

A shopkeeper approached Belle later. "Is it true they will be teaching the village children to read?"

"Yes," Belle replied. "They'll start this week."

"We only have one doctor," the man added quietly. "And he's losing his eyesight."

Belle nodded. "I know."

His voice lowered. "These new professionals—are they for the village?"

"Yes," Belle said, meeting his gaze. "Primarily."

That answer surprised him.

Over the next hour, questions flowed—some sincere, some edged with fear.

"Will Henry send more teachers?"
"Perhaps," Belle answered. "If need continues and progress shows."

"And the children?" a woman asked. "They'll go to school?"

"They already are," Belle said. "Here. In the village. Reading, writing, numbers."

The wagon sold steadily.

Elizabeth closed the ledger at the end of the stop, eyes bright. "They made more today than last week."

Belle smiled. "Consistency builds confidence."

As the train whistle sounded, Belle gathered the professionals.

"This," she said, gesturing to the platform, "is where you'll help hold the line."

Elizabeth nodded, resolve set. "I understand."

Belle looked at Mateo and Clara. "And you—medicine and teaching. Heal and grow."

They nodded together.

Belle felt the familiar tightening in her chest.

Time.

That evening, she told them.

"I leave tomorrow."

Silence answered.

Clara reached for her hand. "You've done what you came to do."

"Yes," Belle said softly. "And now you will do what you're called to do."

They prayed together—gratitude, courage, protection—laughter breaking through the tears when someone joked that Belle should at least leave forwarding instructions.

"Always," Belle laughed. "In triplicate."

The train felt familiar—like a chapter resuming mid-sentence.

Belle found her seat, first class again, bags stowed, heart full and steady. As the conductor called out destinations, a familiar voice laughed nearby.

"Well, if it isn't Doctor Belle."

She turned to see Abner Clay, hat tipped just so, eyes warm.

"Abner," she said. "You always show up on time."

"Some folks schedule meetings," he replied. "We get assigned intersections."

They walked a few steps together.

"So," Abner asked, "did the village get its miracle?"

"They did," Belle said. "Several."

He smiled. "Then it'll hold."

They talked—about the wagon, about Elizabeth stepping in, about Mateo and Clara settling. Abner shook his head more than once.

"You leave places stronger than you find them," he said.

Belle shrugged. "I leave when they're ready."

The days passed quickly.

Fields rolled by. Towns flickered. Letters waited in Belle's bag, reminders of the work ahead.

At last, the conductor called her destination.

The platform bustled—clean, orderly, expectant.

A small group waited together: the twin brothers, Silas and Samuel Whitmore, identical in build but not in temperament—one smiling broadly, the other scanning the crowd. Beside them stood Mayor Edwin Caldwell, dignified and curious, hat clasped to his chest. An elderly physician leaned on a cane, eyes sharp despite age—Dr. Horace Lennox. And finally, the sheriff—Thomas Reed—solid, watchful, respectful.

Belle stepped down.

Mayor Caldwell stepped forward. "Doctor Belle?"

"Yes," she replied.

"We're grateful you've arrived," he said. "Our doctor could use relief."

Dr. Lennox smiled wryly. "And instruction."

The twins grinned together.

Sheriff Reed tipped his hat. "Welcome."

Belle looked at their faces—need, readiness, expectation—and felt the quiet certainty settle again.

"Thank you," she said. "I'm ready."

The train pulled away behind her.

Another place.

Another beginning.

And Belle stepped forward—exactly where she was meant to be.

Belle stepped fully onto the platform, feeling the ground steady beneath her feet, the noise of the station settling into a familiar rhythm. The mayor was speaking again—something polite, something official—but Belle felt a shifting in her spirit that made her glance past him.

She had thought she was meant to arrive alone.

She was wrong.

Three women stood just beyond the official welcoming party, positioned carefully as if they did not wish to appear part of the crowd but did not want to miss whatever was unfolding either.

Belle recognized them instantly.

The first woman stood very straight, gloved hands folded tightly at her waist, hat trimmed in lace far too formal for the hour. She had the posture of someone accustomed to respect—and to giving none until it was earned.

Belle remembered her clearly.

She was the woman who had watched from the platform months ago when Belle had been returned to the train by Native Americans after the storm. She had whispered then—just loud enough to wound—about impropriety, about "wandering among savages." She had not offered water. She had not asked if Belle was safe.

She only watched.

The second woman was middle-aged, dressed in somber colors that signaled dignity rather than wealth. Her eyes were sharper than the first—calculating, observant. Belle remembered her too.

She was present the day Belle stepped off the train to attend to the colored man suffering a heart attack. She had clutched her purse more tightly, lips thinning as Abner Clay carried Belle's bag away.

"Well," she had murmured then, "that certainly explains her associations."

The third woman stood apart slightly, younger than the other two but no less certain of herself. Belle remembered her most vividly.

She was the one who had leaned down that day, lowering her voice as if bestowing wisdom.

"You should be careful," she had whispered. "You don't want to catch a disease from them."

Belle had not responded then.

But she remembered.

Now—all three were here.

Waiting.

They watched closely as Mayor Caldwell gestured toward Belle, his voice rising just enough to be heard.

"We are grateful that Dr. Belle has accepted our request and joined us."

The words landed like a bell toll.

All three women stiffened.

The first adjusted her gloves.

The second lifted her chin slightly.

The third blinked—once, twice.

Belle felt it—not vindication, not pride—but recognition.

These women had been witnesses.

Not to gossip.

To obedience they did not understand at the time.

She met their eyes briefly, kindly, without triumph.

Not I told you so.

Simply Yes. It was me.

A quiet murmur rippled outward.

"Dr. Belle?"
"The one from the train?"
"She's the doctor?"

The women exchanged glances—measuring, reassessing, remembering.

259

Belle turned back to the waiting officials, but she knew this was not finished.

This was a reckoning yet to come.

And as she followed Mayor Caldwell toward her new beginning, she thought only this:

Some people must see the whole road before they understand the destination.

She walked forward anyway.

The next chapter was already watching her.

CHAPTER TWENTY-TWO

Belle followed Mayor Caldwell out of the station with measured steps, her carpetbag balanced neatly at her side. She did not hurry. She had learned long ago that arriving calmly often unsettled people more than arriving late.

A polished carriage waited just beyond the platform, dark wood gleaming, brass fittings catching the afternoon sun. The driver stood tall and attentive, reins looped loosely in practiced hands.

"Well," Belle said lightly, eyeing it, "this is considerably more dignified than I'm used to."

Mayor Edwin Caldwell chuckled, adjusting his coat. "We try, Doctor. Appearances matter here."

Beside him, Dr. Horace Lennox leaned carefully on his cane, eyes narrowed and weakened against the glare but still sharp in expression. Sheriff Thomas Reed mounted his horse smoothly, reins steady.

"I'll meet you there," the sheriff said. "Figured you'd prefer the carriage."

"I appreciate the thought," Belle replied. "My knees do as well."

They set off together—carriage rolling forward, the sheriff pacing them on horseback, the town unfolding in neat rows as they traveled.

Mayor Caldwell cleared his throat, clearly eager.

"We're very glad you've finally come," he said. "It's been almost a year since our first correspondence."

"Yes," Belle replied mildly. "Life has… intervened."

Dr. Lennox snorted softly. "That much is clear."

The mayor continued, voice careful. "I'll be direct, Doctor Belle. We were hoping for a male physician."

Belle smiled faintly. "Of course you were."

"But," Caldwell rushed on, "given Dr. Lennox's eyesight—no offense intended—and the lack of alternatives, we're grateful you accepted."

Dr. Lennox turned his head toward her. "Offense would require energy," he said dryly. "And I'm saving mine for teaching you where the skeletons are buried. Figuratively, of course."

Belle laughed, genuine and warm. "That may be the most honest welcome I've had."

They reached her cottage moments later.

It was small but charming—whitewashed walls, a tidy garden, smoke curling gently from a newly built chimney. Functional, not ornamental.

"This is yours," Caldwell said. "Prepared in anticipation of your arrival."

Belle stepped down and surveyed it with approval. "It's perfect."

Sheriff Reed dismounted and joined them.

"Now," Belle said briskly, "let's discuss duties."

That caught them slightly off guard.

"I'll need to know," she continued, "whether there's an official office space for daily practice, or if house calls will be the norm."

Caldwell blinked. "Ah—well—"

"I can drive a wagon," Belle added. "And ride a horse. But I prefer a covered wagon and a team if I'm expected to travel daily."

Dr. Lennox smiled broadly. "I like her already."

"That can be arranged," Caldwell said quickly. "A wagon will be delivered this afternoon."

"And staff?" Belle continued smoothly. "Someone to cook and clean a few days a week would be helpful. I prefer my energy directed at patients, not scrubbing floors."

"Yes, yes," Caldwell nodded. "That's acceptable."

"And salary?" Belle asked.

The carriage seemed suddenly very quiet.

"Well," Caldwell said carefully, "the amount must be sanctioned by the town."

Belle raised an eyebrow. "A committee?"

"Technically," he said.

"And when do they meet?"

"Tonight," Caldwell replied.

Belle smiled. "Excellent."

Sheriff Reed frowned slightly. "Doctor, you don't mind?"

"Not at all," Belle said serenely. "It's taxpayer money. I respect accountability."

Dr. Lennox laughed. "She's going to cause trouble."

"Order," Belle corrected pleasantly.

They arranged the rest quickly.

A wagon would be brought by dusk. Directions to the town hall given. A woman would be sent later in the week to assist with household tasks.

As they prepared to depart, Caldwell hesitated.

"Doctor Belle," he said, "you should know—the town can be… particular."

Belle smiled kindly. "So am I."

She watched them leave, then stepped inside her cottage and set her bag down.

"Lord," she prayed softly, "I suspect tonight will be educational."

The town hall was full well before Belle arrived.

People lined the walls, packed into rows, perched on windowsills. Voices buzzed with speculation.

"She's the one from the train."
"A woman doctor."
"I heard she lived with Indians."

Belle entered calmly, her posture composed, eyes observant.

At the front sat three women, unmistakably prepared.

Mrs. Adeline Worthington, elegant and severe, gloved hands folded tightly.
Mrs. Prudence Hawthorne, middle-aged, sharp-eyed, lips pursed.
Miss Eleanor Whitby, younger, impeccably dressed, chin lifted in practiced disdain.

Belle recognized them.

They recognized her.

Mayor Caldwell struck his gavel.

"We are gathered," he began, "to welcome Dr. Belle and to discuss her role and compensation."

Dr. Lennox stood slowly.

"I praise the Lord," he said clearly, "for sending her. My eyes fail me, but His do not."

A murmur of approval followed—until it didn't.

A man stood abruptly. "Why couldn't you find a man doctor?"

Another shouted, "Women don't belong in the practice!"

A group of women at the side—the reformed soiled doves—shifted uneasily as eyes turned toward them.

Mrs. Worthington rose gracefully.

"I speak," she said coolly, "for the refined ladies of this town."

Belle folded her hands.

Mrs. Hawthorne joined her. "We object to this woman's presence."

Miss Whitby's voice cut sharp. "She is a danger."

Mayor Caldwell banged the gavel. "Order!"

Mrs. Worthington continued.

"She lived with Native Americans."

"She lived with colored people," Hawthorne added.

"And Mexicans," Whitby concluded.

"They carry diseases," Worthington said crisply. "Deadly ones."

Hawthorne nodded. "She could infect our children."

Miss Whitby sneered. "Once a soiled companion, always unclean."

A hush fell.

Belle stood slowly.

Not defensive.

Not angry.

Just steady.

She did not speak yet.

This—she knew—was not the moment.

This was the reveal.

The reckoning would come next.

And as murmurs rose again, Belle lifted her eyes heavenward for a split second.

"Jesus," she whispered under her breath, "You always know when to let truth wait."

The mayor raised his gavel again, face pale.

"This meeting," he said shakily, "will continue."

And so would the conflict.

Belle was not surprised.

Hurt? A little.
Amused? More than she should have been.
Surprised? Not at all.

The moment she saw those three women sitting in the front row—Adeline Worthington, Prudence Hawthorne, and Eleanor Whitby—Belle had known that something was going to explode. Refinement, she'd discovered, often carried a short fuse.

That was why she had prayed before she came. Knees on the floor of her little cottage, hands folded, heart steady.

"Jesus," she had said, "give me Your words or give me silence. And if I must choose, let it be silence until You are ready."

Now, standing in the town hall as accusations flew, she could almost feel that earlier prayer wrapped around her shoulders like a shawl.

She listened.

She let them say it all.

She lived with Native Americans.
She lived with colored people.
She lived with Mexicans.
She might "carry diseases."
She was "unclean by association."
She would "contaminate the town."

The reformed soiled doves shifted nervously in their seats, shoulders curling in reflex from years of condemnation. When the refined women hissed, "Once a spoiled dove, always a spoiled dove," Belle saw the entire group wince as if struck.

The mayor hammered his gavel in desperation.

"Order! Order, please!"

The crowd only roared louder.

Finally, perhaps out of exhaustion more than authority, he shouted, "Let Dr. Belle speak!"

The hall stilled—restless, simmering, but quiet enough.

Belle rose.

She did not turn first to the mayor.

Or the men.

Or even to the three refined ladies whose faces wore the same expression as soured milk.

She turned to the reformed soiled doves sitting in the meeting, there was about seven in attendance.

They sat in a cluster—about seven of them in the front row—backs straight, hands clasped tightly in their laps. Their dresses were simple but clean. Faces washed. Hair neat. Souls still bearing scars that only Jesus had seen fully.

Belle met their eyes.

"Ladies," she said gently, "may I ask you a few questions?"

They looked startled. One nodded cautiously. Another murmured, "Yes, ma'am."

"How many of you are there in your mission?" Belle asked.

"Seven in our leadership group," one replied. "But…" She hesitated. "There are two hundred or more women we help."

Belle nodded. "Do you have a mission? A purpose?"

"Yes," another answered, sitting taller. "We help women leave the saloons. We share the Gospel. We find work when we can. We pray with them. We show them they can be more than what people called them."

"And do the women you serve need a doctor?" Belle asked.

A ripple of sad laughter moved through them.

"Yes," the first woman said. "Desperately. Many are sick. Some from hard living. Some from babies lost. Some from things we don't even have words for."

Belle nodded slowly, as if confirming what she already knew.

Then she asked the question Heaven had placed on her tongue.

"In front of this entire town," she said clearly, voice steady, "would you—would your mission—welcome me as your doctor?"

The answer came faster than breath.

They jumped to their feet.

"Yes!"

"Yes, we would!"

"Yes, Doctor, please!"

The hall shook with the force of their response.

Belle turned now—finally—to the front where Mayor Caldwell stood, gavel frozen midair, eyes wide. Dr. Lennox looked troubled and exhausted. Sheriff Reed watched carefully, unreadable.

"I don't want your job," Belle said calmly to the mayor. "Nor your so-called 'welcoming committee' of refined ladies."

A shocked gasp ran through the hall.

She turned back to the reformed doves and smiled.

"Lead the way."

For a moment, the entire room forgot how to breathe.

Then the place erupted.

Men shouted. Women whispered. One of the refined ladies gasped loud enough to echo off the rafters. Someone muttered, "Well, I never!" which made Belle suspect they actually had—but only in ways that were socially approved.

Belle did not argue with anyone.

She simply walked.

The seven reformed doves stepped into the aisle, linking arms with her—one on each side, the others behind, forming a protective cluster of former shame walking in present purpose.

They walked out of that hall arm in arm.

Not sneaking.

Not slinking.

Not apologizing.

Going forward.

The gavel pounded helplessly behind them.

"They'll regret this!" one man shouted.

"Then let the three prominent ladies' doctor you all!" another called back.

That earned scattered, nervous laughter.

Outside, the night air felt fresher.

One of the reformed doves—a tall woman with auburn hair pinned neatly—turned to Belle with tears brimming.

"Doctor," she whispered, "you just walked away from their approval."

Belle smiled. "I never applied for it."

They laughed then—real laughter, released like a held breath.

And together, they walked toward the mission.

The reformatory—or "mission house," as the women called it—rose at the end of a quiet street, set slightly apart from the main bustle of the town.

It was not what Belle expected.

It was better.

A wide, two-story building with clean white siding, front steps freshly swept, and flower boxes hung beneath every window. A simple wooden cross hung above the door—no gilt, no ornament, just plain wood polished by careful hands.

Inside, the air smelled of soap, bread, and something else Belle recognized instantly: hope that had been allowed to unpack its bags.

Women moved through the halls—not rushing, but purposeful. Some carried laundry. Others scrubbed floors. A few sat at tables reading from well-worn Bibles. Each woman wore a simple dress and an expression somewhere between weary and determined.

"How many women live here?" Belle asked softly.

"About two hundred," one of the leaders replied. "Some stay a few weeks. Some stay months. A few years… some never leave. This is home now."

They led her into a large common room where a group of women were gathered in a circle—praying, singing softly, some just sitting close enough to feel less alone.

At the front stood the mission director, a woman in her fifties with strong shoulders and kind eyes.

"Doctor Belle," one of the leaders announced, "this is Sister Miriam Caldwell."

Belle blinked. "Caldwell?"

The woman smiled knowingly. "The mayor's older sister," she said. "We do not always see eye to eye. But we do share a childhood."

That made Belle laugh.

Sister Miriam stepped forward and took both of Belle's hands.

"We have been praying for you," she said. "We didn't know your name. We only knew we needed a doctor who feared God more than social circles."

Belle felt tears prick her eyes.

"Well," she said, "you certainly got that."

Someone said, "Praise the Lord!" and the rest quickly echoed, "Amen!"

"It's the town's loss," Sister Miriam added firmly. "But it is our gain. And we serve the same Jesus, so we will not complain."

A murmur of agreement rippled through the women.

They showed Belle the dormitories—rows of neatly made beds, trunks at the foot of each. A small chapel. A modest kitchen where women knelt to pull bread from the oven. A tiny sewing room where work was done to keep the mission afloat.

"We do our best," Sister Miriam said. "But our bodies… our histories… have taken a toll. We need medical care—real care. Not just tonics from the general store."

"You have it now," Belle replied. "As much as my two hands and one brain can provide."

Sister Miriam chuckled. "That'll be more than we've ever had."

Then one of the leaders spoke hesitantly.

"There is something more," she said.

"Ask," Belle replied.

"We try to help the girls still working in the saloons," the woman said. "They come to us sick sometimes. Or after a beating. Or when a baby is coming and they don't know what to do."

Another woman added, "Some are afraid to leave yet. But they're not afraid to be seen by a doctor."

"Would you… tend to them too?" Sister Miriam asked.

Belle didn't hesitate.

"Yes," she said. "I will."

They let out a breath collectively, as if they'd been holding it for months.

"And," Belle added with a small grin, "I will dress fancy when I go."

They stared.

"Fancy?" one repeated.

"Yes," Belle said. "If I walk in there looking like a sermon, they'll brace themselves. But if I walk in looking like I'm simply visiting as one woman to another, they might listen."

One of the women laughed. "Doctor Belle, you're going to out-dress the madam."

Belle shrugged. "Scripture says we should be wise as serpents and harmless as doves. I figure a well-placed ribbon falls under wisdom."

They laughed harder at that.

Later that night, as the town erupted in argument—half saying, "Good riddance to her," and the other half muttering, "Then let those three ladies' doctor you when you're sick".

Candles flickered.

Voices from the common room in the mission drifted in—prayer, singing, soft conversation.

Sister Miriam bowed her head.

"Lord," she prayed, "thank You for sending this doctor where others turned her away. Thank You that You take what people reject and plant it where it will bear much fruit."

Belle added quietly, "And thank You that You walk straight through man-made reputations and call people by their real names."

They stood there in companionable silence for a while.

Then Belle smiled.

"Well," she said, "it appears I have unexpected patients."

"And," Sister Miriam replied with a twinkle in her eye, "an entire town watching to see what you do next."

Belle chuckled. "Good. Maybe they'll see Jesus while they're at it."

Outside, the town was split.

Inside, the mission was united.

And Belle knew: this had not been a rejection.

It was a redirection—right into the middle of the very people Jesus loved to surprise.

At the end of the night, when the lamps were finally lowered and the sounds of the mission settled into a familiar hush, Belle stood alone for a moment near the open doorway.

The air was cool.
The stars were clear.
Laughter drifted softly from somewhere down the hall, mingled with quiet prayer and the steady breathing of rest.

No gavel.
No accusations.
No explanations required.

She pressed her palm lightly against the doorframe—solid, real, welcoming—and felt something settle in her spirit that the long road had never quite allowed before.

Not duty.
Not endurance.
Not resilience.

Belonging.

She exhaled slowly, a smile touching her lips, and whispered, almost to herself,

"Halleluiah! *I am finally home*"

1890 RECIPES

NATIVE AMERICAN

- Three Sisters Stew
- Wild Berry Corn Mash
- Pemmican
- Hominy with Ash Water

ROMANI (GYPSY)

- Campfire Potato & Onion Skillet
- Ash Flat Bread
- Fire-Roasted Cabbage & Carrots
- Milk-Soaked Bread

BLACK FRONTIER

- Sorghum Cornbread
- Slow Greens with Salt Meat
- Sweet Potato Mash

MEXICAN FRONTIER

- Beans with Chili & Garlic
- Hand-Pat Corn Tortillas

BELLE'S HEALER KITCHEN (CROSS-CULTURAL)

- Bone Broth

- Milk & Honey Porridge

NATIVE AMERICAN–INSPIRED RECIPES

(Simple, nourishing, healing-centered foods Belle would have learned while traveling)

1. Three Sisters Stew (Corn, Beans, Squash)

A sustaining dish shared across many tribes

Ingredients

- Dried corn kernels or cracked corn
- Dried beans (pinto or black)
- Winter squash or pumpkin, cubed
- Water
- Animal fat or bear grease (or lard)

Instructions

1. Soak beans overnight near the fire.
2. Boil beans in fresh water until tender.
3. Add corn and cubed squash.
4. Simmer slowly until thick.
5. Stir in a small amount of fat before serving.

Purpose in Story:
A food Belle would give the sick—high strength, gentle digestion.

2. Wild Berry Corn Mash

Eaten warm during recovery

Ingredients

- Cornmeal
- Dried berries (blueberry, chokecherry, or serviceberry)
- Water

Instructions

1. Boil water.
2. Stir in cornmeal slowly to avoid lumps.
3. Add berries and cook until soft.
4. Eat warm with a wooden spoon.

Purpose in Story:

Perfect after fever or childbirth scenes.

ROMANI (GYPSY) TRAVELER RECIPES

(Portable, fire-based meals made on the road)

3. Romani Campfire Potato & Onion Skillet

Cheap, filling, and shared

Ingredients

- Potatoes, sliced
- Onion, sliced
- Lard or dripping
- Salt

Instructions

1. Heat fat in a shallow iron pan.
2. Fry onions until soft.
3. Add potatoes and cook until browned.
4. Cover briefly to steam, then uncover to crisp.

Purpose in Story:
Food Belle cooks at wagon camps—humble but grounding.

4. Flat Camp Bread (Ash Bread)

No yeast, no oven

Ingredients

- Flour
- Water
- Salt

Instructions

1. Mix into stiff dough.
2. Shape into flat rounds.
3. Place on hot stones or in ashes.
4. Turn once until firm and browned.

Purpose in Story:
Bread Belle breaks with travelers before prayer.

BLACK (COLORED) FRONTIER & CHURCH COOKING

(Soul-sustaining foods tied to dignity, survival, and faith)

5. Sorghum Cornbread

Common in Black homesteads and church kitchens

Ingredients

- Cornmeal
- Sorghum molasses
- Lard
- Water or milk

Instructions

1. Mix cornmeal with warm liquid.
2. Stir in sorghum and fat.
3. Bake in a greased skillet until firm.

Purpose in Story:
Used when Belle feeds working families or church gatherings.

6. Slow Greens with Salt Meat

A dish of patience

Ingredients

- Collard or mustard greens
- Salt pork or smoked meat
- Water

Instructions

1. Boil meat gently.
2. Add washed greens.
3. Simmer several hours until tender.

Purpose in Story:
Comfort food for grief, endurance, and long evenings.

MEXICAN FRONTIER RECIPES

(Borderland cooking common in Texas, New Mexico, and the Southwest)

7. Beans with Chili and Garlic

Peasant food, deeply nourishing

Ingredients

- Dried beans
- Garlic
- Dried chili pods
- Lard
- Water

Instructions

1. Soak beans overnight.
2. Boil until soft.
3. Fry garlic and crushed chili in lard.
4. Stir into beans and simmer.

8. Corn Tortillas (Hand-Patted)

Daily bread of the people

Ingredients

- Cornmeal or masa
- Water
- Salt

Instructions

1. Mix into soft dough.
2. Pat thin with hands.
3. Cook on a hot iron griddle until spotted.

Purpose in Story:
Used when Belle feeds mothers and children.

CROSS-CULTURAL HEALING FOODS (BELLE'S KITCHEN)

9. Bone Broth for the Weak

Doctor's food

Ingredients

- Beef or chicken bones
- Onion
- Water

Instructions

1. Simmer bones for several hours.
2. Strain.
3. Serve hot with bread.

Purpose:
After injury, childbirth, fever.

10. Milk & Honey Porridge

Given to the exhausted

Ingredients

- Milk
- Oats or cornmeal
- Honey or molasses

Instructions

1. Simmer grain in milk.
2. Sweeten lightly.
3. Serve warm.

Purpose:
Recovery and comfort scenes.

I. NATIVE AMERICAN HEALING & TRAVEL FOODS

(Rooted in preservation, energy, and communal survival)

11. Pemmican (Travel & Emergency Food)

Authenticity: Plains tribes; widely shared during long journeys

Ingredients

- Dried lean meat (bison, venison, or beef)
- Rendered animal fat
- Dried berries (optional)

Instructions

1. Pound dried meat into fine shreds.
2. Warm rendered fat until liquid.
3. Mix meat and fat thoroughly.
4. Add berries if available.
5. Press into small cakes and allow to harden.

Story Use:
Belle carries this during overland travel or gives it to those fleeing famine or illness. No spoilage. No waste.

12. Hominy with Ash Water

Authenticity: Southeastern & Plains tribes

Ingredients

- Dried corn kernels
- Ash water (from hardwood ashes)
- Water

Instructions

1. Soak corn in ash water overnight.
2. Rinse repeatedly.
3. Boil until kernels swell and soften.

Story Use:
Taught to Belle as **nutritionally transformative food**—a moment of cultural exchange and respect.

ROMANI (GYPSY) ROAD & CARAVAN COOKING

(Foods meant to be cooked fast, shared freely, and stretched)

13. Fire-Roasted Cabbage and Carrots

Authenticity: Eastern European Romani influence

Ingredients

- Cabbage wedges
- Carrots
- Salt
- Fat drippings

Instructions

1. Place vegetables directly near hot coals.
2. Turn slowly until edges char.
3. Drizzle with fat and sprinkle salt.

Story Use:
Cooked quickly during camp stops, symbolizing mobility and independence.

14. Milk-Soaked Bread with Honey

Authenticity: Romani & traveling poor

Ingredients

- Day-old bread
- Milk
- Honey or molasses

Instructions

1. Warm milk gently.
2. Pour over bread.
3. Sweeten lightly.

Story Use:
Fed to children or the ill when nothing else is available—
kindness without ceremony.

BLACK FRONTIER & POST-EMANCIPATION SURVIVAL COOKING

(Foods passed down through resilience and ingenuity)

15. Sweet Potato Mash with Fatback

Authenticity: Southern Black homesteads & camps

Ingredients

- Sweet potatoes
- Fatback or salt pork

Instructions

1. Roast or boil sweet potatoes.
2. Mash thoroughly.
3. Stir in rendered fatback.

Story Use:
Belle prepares this after hard labor days—**strength without extravagance**.

HOW TO START A CHRISTIAN BOOK CLUB

Begin with prayer and clarity of purpose. Decide whether the book club exists for fellowship, discipleship, outreach, or community rebuilding. A clear purpose helps guide discussion and direction.

Choose a simple, accessible meeting place such as a home, church room, library, café, community center, or park. Consistency matters more than size or appearance.

Select one book and set expectations for reading pace. Decide how many chapters will be read per meeting and how often the group will gather.

Invite people who are open, curious, or seeking. A Christian book club should feel safe for honest questions and different stages of faith.

Set basic expectations such as respect, confidentiality, and listening without interruption. Make it clear that no one is required to have all the answers.

Open meetings with prayer. Read together. Use discussion questions instead of lectures. Close with prayer or reflection.

Allow the group to grow naturally. Focus on relationships first, trusting that spiritual fruit develops over time.

HOW TO START A FARMERS MARKET

Begin by defining the mission of the farmers market. Decide whether it exists to provide fresh food, support local growers, create jobs, restore a neighborhood, or build community.

Choose a visible and manageable location such as a church parking lot, community garden, vacant space with permission, school grounds, or a public park.

Connect with local farmers, gardeners, bakers, cooks, and artisans. Start small with people you trust and expand as interest grows.

Confirm local requirements such as permits, food safety rules, vendor guidelines, and liability coverage. Many grassroots markets operate successfully under a church or nonprofit umbrella.

Set a consistent schedule, such as weekly or twice monthly. Reliability helps the community plan and participate.

Create a welcoming atmosphere where families feel safe and valued. Hospitality matters more than perfection.

Prioritize service over profit. A market rooted in care for people tends to grow naturally and sustainably

THE SINNER'S PRAYER

Jesus, I believe You are the Son of God. I believe You died for my sins and rose again. I confess that I have sinned and cannot save myself. I ask You to forgive me and cleanse me completely. I turn away from my old life and turn toward You. Come into my heart and be my Lord and Savior. I place my trust in You alone. Thank You for saving me. I choose to follow You from this day forward. In Jesus' name, amen. **WHAT TO DO AFTER THE PRAYER**

Begin speaking to God daily through prayer. Use simple, honest words and allow space to listen. Read the Bible regularly, beginning with the Gospel of John to understand who Jesus is and how He lived.

Connect with other believers through a church, small group, or Christian book club where growth is encouraged and supported. Be baptized when you are ready as a public declaration of faith and obedience.

Allow spiritual growth to happen gradually. Transformation is a process, and grace walks with you through it.

Serve others in practical ways. Faith grows stronger when lived out through action and love.

Trust God with your journey. You do not need all the answers immediately. Take one faithful step at a time

PRAY FOR HEALING

Heavenly Father,
I come before You just as I am. You see my body, my
mind, my emotions, and the places where I am tired,
hurting, or worn down. Nothing in me is hidden from You,
and I thank You that I do not have to pretend to be strong in
Your presence.

Jesus, I acknowledge that You are my Healer. By Your
stripes I have been healed, and I receive that truth now. I
ask You to touch every place in me that needs restoration.
Where there is pain, bring relief. Where there is sickness,
bring wholeness. Where there is inflammation, imbalance,
fear, or exhaustion, bring Your peace and order.

Holy Spirit, search me and show me anything that
needs to be released—unforgiveness, stress, grief, worry, or
hidden burdens. I choose to let them go and place them
fully into Your hands. I receive Your comfort and Your
strength in return.

I speak life over my body. I declare that my cells, my
organs, my systems, and my breath respond to the authority
of Jesus Christ. I choose faith over fear and trust over
uncertainty. Even as healing unfolds, I thank You in
advance for what You are doing now and what You are
completing in Your time.

Lord, help me to rest without guilt, to listen to my body
with wisdom, and to walk in obedience as You guide my

steps. Whether healing comes quickly or gradually, I commit to trusting You fully.

I receive Your peace. I receive Your healing. I receive Your sustaining grace today.
Through the precious blood of Jesus.

In Jesus' name, amen.

The Reformed Soiled Doves Narrative Declaration

We as former **soiled doves openly proclaim** that:

We desire **purity from this point forward.**
We choose to **honor God with their bodies.**
We will **keep ourselves sexually pure until marriage.**

Our past does not define their future.
Our choice is not hidden or whispered—it is **spoken aloud** as testimony.

We do not make this declaration from shame,
but from **conviction, healing, and restored dignity.**

This proclamation becomes part of our story's witness:

- that redemption is real,
- that bodies our can be reclaimed,
- and that holiness is a forward-facing decision.